Superstar

Cathy Hopkins

Million Dollar Mates

Superstar

www.simonandschuster.co.uk
www.simonandschuster.com.au

SIMON AND SCHUSTER

First published in Great Britain in 2013 by Simon and Schuster UK Ltd
A CBS COMPANY

1 3 5 7 9 10 8 6 4 2

Simon & Schuster UK Ltd
1st Floor
222 Gray's Inn Road
London WC1X 8HB

Simon & Schuster Australia, Sydney
Simon & Schuster India, New Delhi

A CIP catalogue record for this book
is available from the British Library.

PB ISBN: 978-0-85707-603-8
EBook ISBN: 978-0-85707-604-5

Printed and bound by CPI Group (UK) Ltd, Croydon, CR0 4YY
www.simonandschuster.co.uk

Superstar

1

Summer Chores

'Now it's the summer holidays, Dad thinks I'm his personal slave,' I said to Pia as we fought our way through a bustling aisle in Harrods food hall. 'Just because he works for No 1, Porchester Park, it doesn't mean I do.'

'Mum's the same,' Pia replied. 'We've just finished our GCSEs, the most stressful time of our lives. You'd think they'd give us some time off to recover.'

'I know. Marie Quigley's mum treated her to a weekend break at a fab spa hotel when she'd finished her last exam,' I said.

'And Carrie Daniel's parents have let her go to

Cornwall with a bunch of mates for the whole of July. But what do we get on our first proper day off? A list of chores.'

'So unfair,' we chorused, then burst out laughing.

'Though Dad did say that he's organising something for me next week,' I said. 'He was being all mysterious.'

'I bet it will be somewhere fab,' said Pia. 'Lucky you.'

'Maybe Cornwall or Italy. I saw him checking out an article about Italy in the Sunday paper.'

'With Charlie?'

'I'd imagine so.'

Pia laughed. 'At least you have your brother for company, unlike me, stuck on my own with my mum for a week in Denmark visiting relatives. It's hardly Glam City, is it?' She suddenly clapped her hand over her mouth. 'Oh, Jess, sorry.'

I put my arm around her and gave her a squeeze. 'Hey, it's fine. You can't censor talking about your mother all the time.' My mum died over a year and a half ago and Pia knows how much I miss her and would give anything to spend some more time with her.

'When I'm back we can all be together again,' said

Pia as we approached the pastry counter. 'That's the bit of the holiday I'm looking forward to most. Hanging out with mates, and with Henry, of course. Just chilling and doing very little.'

'I can't wait to spend some time with JJ,' I said. JJ's my boyfriend of exactly one term plus four days and eighteen hours, not that I'm counting. He is also the son of Jefferson Lewis, the black American A-list movie star. It's still a thrill to be in a relationship with him even though we're not newbies any more. Henry is Pia's boyfriend. He is the son of Mr Sawtell who looks after the cars at No 1, Porchester Park. They've been together since Pia first moved to No 1 when her mum got the job managing the spa area.

Porchester Park is the poshest, most luxurious apartment block in London. The kind of people who live there are the international glitterazzi and super rich. They need to be rich because apartments start at twenty million and go up to one hundred and fifty mill, and are often a second or third home for the residents; the type of people who buy them have other places in the USA or the South of France or the Caribbean as well. My dad is the general manager and, like Pia and her mum, my family lives on site in a mews house. Ours is a very ordinary house, but the

3

location is like nowhere else; when you step from the staff area into the residents' part, it's like walking into wonderland: the air is scented with Jo Malone candles, the floor is made from exquisite Italian marble and the daily flower displays on the table in reception cost more than my pocket money for a year. In other words, everything is the best of the best.

'Actually,' I added, 'JJ texted that he needs to talk to me about the holidays.'

Pia grinned. 'Yay. Remember the last time he texted you with a message like that?'

I nodded. It was to tell me that Pia and I had been invited to go with the Lewis family to Udaipur in India in the Easter holidays. It was the trip of a lifetime and seven-star luxury all the way. I felt a shiver of anticipation. Maybe I would be asked to join JJ and his family in the Hamptons in America or the Caribbean or Hawaii or one of the other exotic locations where they spent their summers.

Being in a couple with JJ is definitely different to dating the local boys. Our relationship has catapulted me into a world of privilege and, at first, I felt intimidated by the luxury and sheer fabulousness of it all. In JJ's world, it's top notch all the way and so different from my normal life. I've adapted now though and no longer feel that I don't belong when I go up to the state-of-the-art apartment where he lives with his parents and sister Alisha, or when I'm in the back of one of the chauffeur-driven limos that takes us around London. When I'm with him, I know that we'll get the best theatre tickets, best table in a restaurant, a personal shopper to greet us when out shopping; basically it all makes me feel really special. I've relaxed a lot since I first met him and now I absolutely love hanging out in his world. I'd be mad not to.

'It's nice and cool in here,' said Pia as we continued our way through the food hall. She sniffed the air. 'And it always smells wonderful – of freshly baked bread and expensive roasted coffee beans.'

'It *is* expensive too. I know the prices.'

'Only the best at Harrods,' said Pia. 'And it's not such a bad place to do our chores. Remember when we first came in here when we were kids and thought we'd stepped into food fairyland with all the counters of cakes and sweets and pastries?' She pointed up at the roof. 'And you don't get chandeliers in most grocery shops.'

Harrods food hall is not your usual supermarket. It's like walking into a food fantasy, a brightly lit palace with every type of delicacy imaginable, from savoury to sweet, sumptuously displayed in glass counters in the different rooms. Plus there are all the bars to sit and eat sushi or tapas or get a coffee and cake while you watch the busy shoppers go by.

I nodded. 'I thought it was like Willy Wonka's chocolate factory but with more choice. Though now we're fifteen, I prefer the make-up and perfume counters.'

'I still like the cupcake section. It's yum heaven over there,' Pia said as she eyed up a beautiful display of mini cakes with swirled pink and purple icing. She began to read the list. 'Banana. Mocha. Strawberry. Rocky Road. Sticky Toffee. Ooh, I'm getting hungry.'

'Would you shop here if you were rich?'

'How rich?'

'Totally.'

Pia laughed. 'If I was *totally* rich, I'd own Harrods and so wouldn't need to shop here. It would all be mine and I'd just come and take what I wanted.'

I laughed. Pia's answer summed her attitude to life up exactly. She might be small in size at five foot three, but she's big in personality and ambitions. I, on the other hand, am tall at five foot nine, but not nearly as confident as her – like, she's never fazed at all by the rich or famous people who live at

Porchester Park while it took me a while not to feel starstruck. If I'm honest, I still am by some of them when they waft by on their way out, leaving a trace of cologne or perfume in the air, the women in designer silks, the men in handmade suits and shoes. But 'Money can't buy everything,' Pia always says.

'I was hoping to get out and do a bit of sunbathing in the park this afternoon but no chance of that,' I said. 'It's going to take ages to get all this stuff.'

'Come on, let's get our jobs done then we can phone Henry and JJ and hang out. What's next on the list?'

I glanced down at the sheet of paper that Dad had given me earlier in the morning. 'Raspberry and cassis jam,' I said and pointed at an aisle to our left. 'Down there. We should also get a couple of notepads to do the project Mrs Callahan set us.'

Mrs Callahan is our headmistress and gave all of Year Eleven a project to think about over the summer. In our last assembly she'd said, 'As many of you will be coming back here to do A-levels, I want you to spend some of your holiday thinking about your future, who you really are and what are your goals and aspirations. I also want you to think about where happiness lies for you. Get a notebook and jot down thoughts relating to these two things, even if it's just random words. Who am I? Who do I want to be? What is happiness to me? In the autumn, we'll look at them together. I believe they'll help you decide where you want to go in life and what to study at university.'

'I know it's only the start of the holidays,' I said, 'but it won't hurt to get a headstart.'

Pia nodded, then took the paper out of my hand and read the list. 'You get the jam and I'll get the white truffle purée, then we can go together to choose our notepads. Does your dad pay you for the errands he asks you to do for the residents, like a summer job?'

I shook my head. 'As if. He says it's earning my pocket money.'

'Bummer,' said Pia. 'At least Mum pays me a bit extra.' She looked over to the next counter on our right where there was a tall, striking-looking lady with shoulder-length silver hair waiting to be served. Pia did a double take. 'Ohmigod! Isn't that Stephanie Harper?'

'Who's she?'

'Duh. Don't you read your horoscope? She's only the most famous astrologer in the world. She's American but on telly over here all the time – on all the chat shows. She's brilliant and so accurate.' She turned away. 'Oops, mustn't stare.'

Since living at No 1, Porchester Park, we've both had it drummed into us by our parents not to gawp at famous people. We've learnt that the kind of people who live there highly value their privacy. However, I could see Stephanie in the mirror on the wall opposite so could watch without her realising. For a brief second, she glanced up at the mirror, so I pretended I was checking out my reflection. 'Be cool, Pia. She might have seen us staring,' I whispered. We immediately went into our acting casual act. I flicked my hair back. 'Er ... Do you think I should cut my hair for the summer?' I asked in an attempt to look as though staring at Stephanie was the last thing I was doing.

Pia shook her head. 'No. It suits you long. I might even grow mine.' Pia has worn her hair short and spiky for the last year. It suits her because it emphasises her pixie-like features. 'OK, she's paying the assistant. Undercover celebrity watch, recommence.' She turned around and sneaked another look. 'Great necklace. Check it out. And she always wears that peacock-blue shade of her dress. It's like her signature colour.'

I glanced around in my best nonchalant manner. Pia and I have perfected the art for when we want to look at boys but don't want them to know that we're looking at them. It's a slow head turn, taking in the whole room, as if not focusing on anything special when actually we know exactly what we want to look at. With her silver hair, Stephanie really stood out from the crowd as someone with her own style. She was dressed in a calf-length dress, her sandals and bag in a darker shade of blue-green to her dress and at her feet was a gorgeous briefcase in blue snakeskin. It looked like it cost a fortune but what pulled my attention the most was her jewellery. It was all silver – thick bracelets on both wrists, earrings set with aquamarines and a huge aquamarine stone in silver around her neck. She had the look of a high priestess or glamorous elf queen from *Lord of the Rings*. She also had lots of carrier bags, as if she'd been doing some serious shopping and was struggling to pick them all up and walk away.

Suddenly I felt someone else watching me and, through the mirror, a girl in the crowd behind Stephanie caught my eye. A teenager with glossy red hair. I felt myself freeze but tried not to show my reaction. It was Keira Oakley, I was sure it was, but she turned quickly and went the other way. My stomach churned. I'd had a horrible time with Keira earlier in the year when she went out of her way to make my life miserable. We were both entrants in a modelling competition and she did her best to ruin my chances as well as steal my crush back then, Tom Robertson, from under my nose.

'What's the matter?' asked Pia. 'You've gone pale.'

'Don't look round. I thought I saw Keira.'

Pia looked round immediately and scanned the hall. 'I can't see her.'

I glanced back. I couldn't see her either. 'Maybe I imagined it.'

'Hope so,' said Pia. 'That girl makes the mean girls look like angels.'

Pia went off to get the purée and I made my way to the same counter where Stephanie had just been. As I stood there, I noticed her briefcase was still on the floor. I tried to let the assistant know but he was busy down the other end serving another customer. I stood on my tiptoes to see if I could see Stephanie. Luckily, she hadn't left the hall and was over at the cupcake counter. I picked up the case and approached her.

'Er, excuse me,' I said. 'You left your case by the counter.'

Ms Harper stared at me for a few seconds as if not taking in what I was saying. Close up, she was even more striking, her eyes a pale turquoise-blue that matched the stone in her necklace. She gasped and grabbed the case from me. 'Oh my Lord!' she exclaimed in an American accent. 'Idiot. Me, I mean, not you. Heavens. I'd lose my own head if it wasn't screwed on. Thank you. Thank you so much. Say, how did you know it was mine?'

'Oh! I ... My friend and I noticed you. Your clothes. You wear great colours, like the sky and sea. We're ... er ... into fashion.'

'Like the sky and sea, huh?' Ms Harper reached for her purse and drew out a twenty-pound note. 'Here. Get yourself something on me.'

I shook my head. 'No. Really, it's not necessary. I was glad to help. I mean, glad to give it back to you.'

She took out another note. 'Sorry. Of course twenty's not enough. Here.'

Even though there were a million things I could buy with forty pounds, I shook my head again. I didn't feel it would be right to take her money.

'Honestly. I'm just glad to give it back to you. Anyone could have taken it.'

'Exactly and you didn't,' said Ms Harper. 'But if you're sure, thank you. It's good to know that there are some honest people about.'

'You're welcome. Um, bye then.'

'Bye, honey. And you have a good day.'

I moved away and she went back to her shopping. It felt good to have returned her case. *I might put that on my 'What makes me happy' list,* I thought. *A good deed a day!*

After I'd got everything on Dad's list, I met up with Pia again and we caught a glimpse of Ms Harper staggering out of the shop, weighed down by her pile of bags. 'Do you think we should go and help her?' I asked.

Pia shook her head. 'I wouldn't worry. She's probably got a chauffeur waiting by the door. No, let's go and try perfumes then look at the notebooks. We deserve a bit of us time.'

We wandered into the biggest of the perfume halls. I love it in there because it looks like the interior of an Egyptian temple and the air is thick with scent from the many on offer – a heady mix of tuber rose, jasmine, sandalwood and so many I couldn't name. I glanced at the rows and counters with boxes and bottles of Armani, Hermes, Floris, Miller Harris, Annick

Goutal and endless others. A sales assistant came towards us and urged us to try the latest by Valentino. We obliged; it smelt of violets, heady and exotic. We walked on and soon another assistant had sprayed a new Van Cleef and Arpels on our wrists; it had a lighter aroma of freshly cut grass with a woody base note.

'Hmm, lovely,' I said.

'You have to let it settle,' said Pia and pulled me on towards one of the stalls where I squirted some Marc Jacobs, Daisy on to my wrist.

'I know,' I said. 'They all smell gorgeous then you have to wait to see if they mix with your body chemistry. It's amazing, isn't it, how different perfumes smell totally different on different people?'

Pia nudged me. 'Don't look now but danger alert. Eleven o'clock on the Lacoste counter. Turn around and walk away.' She put on a clipped, strict voice. 'Step away from the perfumes, Ms Hall, step away from the perfumes.'

I flashed a look around. Too late. It was Keira. She'd seen us and was coming over. I didn't know whether to run or stay still. My legs decided for me and stayed rooted to the spot. I hate not getting on with people and I hate confrontation. Keira had been so out of order the last time I'd seen her that I'd sworn that I never wanted to have anything to do with her again but here she was, standing right in front of me, smiling her fake smile. My mind went into meltdown. I didn't know how to act. To be friendly would be false but I didn't want to cause a scene in the middle of Harrods either.

'Pia, Jess, how lovely to see you,' gushed Keira. She was a stunning-looking girl with a heart-shaped face and eyes the colour of a cold blue sea. She would have had a good chance in the modelling competition if she hadn't been caught cheating – stealing my dress for the final show to be precise.

'I wish I could say the same,' said Pia, who was never afraid to show her true feelings. 'Come on, Jess, we're going.' She linked my arm and pulled me away.

Keira's face fell. 'Oh. OK. I ... I can't blame you. And I guess I owe you an apology. I'm sorry, Jess, truly I am.'

'Sometimes sorry isn't good enough,' said Pia and tried to pull me away again. 'And anyway, it's a bit late.'

'Jess can speak for herself, Pia,' said Keira. 'Listen. I was in a bad place earlier this year. I wasn't myself, not at all. I don't know whether you know or not but I suffer from depression. I've been getting help and I realised I behaved badly with you. I wanted to get in touch but ... I wasn't sure how you'd react. I'm glad I've bumped into you so I can apologise in person,' she said, and for once she did look sincere.

Pia tugged on my arm. My mind was still spinning. Part of me wanted to say, 'Stay out of my life and don't come near me ever again,' and another part felt sorry for her – and she *had* apologised.

'OK. Fine,' said Pia. 'You're sorry and now we have to go.'

Suddenly Keira sniffed the air. 'I love trying on these perfumes, don't you? What have you been trying?'

'Er ... Daisy,' I muttered. 'All sorts actually.'

Keira picked up the Marc Jacobs tester, pressed the nozzle and the sweet aroma filled the air.

'Ow,' spluttered Pia. Keira had sprayed the scent right into her eyes.

'Oh no! Ohmi*god*,' cried Keira and quickly put the spray down. 'I didn't mean to do that. I *didn't*. I really didn't. The nozzles are so tiny, I didn't realise what direction it was going in. Oh God, you're not going to believe me, are you? Pia, I'm so sorry. Are you OK?'

This time, Pia tugged harder on my arm. 'Just stay away from us, Keira,' she said.

'Jess, *Jess*, you have to believe me. I wouldn't do that on purpose,' she pleaded. 'I was *trying* to apologise, Jess. I really was.'

I wanted to believe her but the sincere look had disappeared and something in her eyes told me she was having a great laugh at our expense.

2

Unexpected News

As soon as Pia and I got back to my house, we settled down with glasses of elderflower cordial at the breakfast bar in the open kitchen and got stuck into the task that Mrs Callahan had set us.

Who am I? I wrote on the first page of my new silver notebook. What is happiness? I added.

'I suppose our choice of notebooks says something about who we are,' Pia commented as she opened her shiny pink one.

'Yes. You're pink, girly and shallow and I'm deep and mysterious.'

Pia biffed my arm. 'So what should we write?'

'I'm going to write a good deed a day gives the feel-good factor,' I said. 'I felt great when I handed Stephanie Harper's case back to her earlier on.'

'I would have felt even happier if you'd accepted the reward,' said Pia. 'We could have gone to the Topshop sale.'

'I couldn't,' I said. 'I would have felt mean.'

'Goody two-shoes,' teased Pia.

'OK, I'll write that under who I am. A Goody two-shoes. Otherwise, we could start with basic stuff, couldn't we?'

Pia nodded. 'We could do it like we do characters in creative writing. Physical, sociological, psychological.'

'Good idea,' I said, and started writing.

<u>Physical</u>
Name: Jessica Hall.
Age: Fifteen.
Birthday: December 3rd.
Appearance: Tall, chestnut hair, blue eyes, slim build. BIG nose.

Pia glanced at what I'd written. 'You don't have a big nose,' she said.

'Do. A great big hooter,' I said.

Pia rolled her eyes then leant over and crossed out *big*. 'Your nose is just the right size for your face. And you have a great mouth, write that down. Wide and often smiling.'

'I can't put that. It will sound like I'm a big-head.' I glanced at what she'd written and burst out laughing. Under physical, she'd put, *small in size but not in personality* (which is true). *Unconventionally good-looking with great sense of personal style* (also true). 'Add big-head,' I said.

Pia shook her head. 'There's a difference between having confidence in who you are and being a big-head. You need to have more confidence. You're one of the best-looking girls at our school and yet you always find fault with yourself – like writing you've got a big nose.'

'Yes, but that is part of what makes me me and what makes you you. You've always been more confident and I've always been less so.' I went back to my notebook and started the next section.

<u>Sociological</u>
Lives at No 1, Porchester Park in a mews house in the staff area. Three bedrooms and an open-plan sitting

room/dining room/kitchen downstairs.
Colour of bedroom: Pale blue.
Family: Lives with brother, Charlie, aged
seventeen. Dad, Michael, and Dave my
black-and-white cat. Mum, deceased.
Others: Gran. Aunt Maddie. Uncle
John and Aunt Cissie and cousins, Sam
and Louis.
Friends: Pia Carlsen. Alisha Lewis. Flo
and Meg.
Boyfriend: JJ Lewis. (It made me feel
great to write that.)
Good at: Art, English, swimming,
daydreaming.

'I don't know what to write for goals,' I said.

Pia spread her arms wide. 'To conquer the world and do something brilliant. Don't hold back or limit yourself.'

'OK,' I said and began to write again.

Goals: Win the Nobel peace prize for
curing cancer. Write a best-selling
novel. Win the gold medal for swimming
in the Olympics. Travel the world. Stay

friends with Pia for all my life.
(It felt good not to limit myself!)

'Let's take a break and read our horoscopes,' said Pia after a short while. 'Got any magazines with them in?'

I quickly scribbled *Sagittarius* in my notebook under starsign. 'Not new ones. These days I usually check out my horoscope in the glossies up at Alisha's. They always have the new *Vogue* and *Harper's* up there.' I indicated the fridge. 'More juice, madam?'

Pia nodded. 'Look on the Internet then. I know, why don't you Google Stephanie Harper and find her site?'

I went to Dad's laptop, which he always keeps on the breakfast bar, and soon found Stephanie's site. Pia got some more elderflower cordial from the fridge, poured two glasses and handed me one. 'Hey, there's a picture here of Stephanie with a teenage boy. Do you think he's her son?' I said.

Pia looked at the screen. 'Probably. He's too young to be her boyfriend, looks about eighteen. Kind of cute in a boho-geek way, isn't he?'

I laughed. Pia was always coming up with new types of boy. Boho geek wasn't one I'd heard before but the

boy on the screen did look interesting, with his mop
of tousled blond hair and the same turquoise eyes as
his mother.

'OK, our July horoscopes. You first, Pia. Ms Aries.
During the summer, it is probably best if you do everything your best friend wants and give her your new
red top.'

Pia didn't blink an eye. 'And what does it really
say?'

'"*Travel abroad is likely and the full moon in Cancer
will make you over-emotional around the eighteenth and
prone to leap before you look with regard to some relationships. Try and stay steady, breathe and take things
slowly.*" Sounds like good advice for you.'

'Huh, as if,' said Pia. 'She's right about the travel
though. Denmark with Mum. What's yours?'

I clicked on the link for Sagittarius and read it out.
'"*Your dreams may meet with some obstacles in the next
week and plans will be disrupted. I see an unexpected
journey. Travel.*"'

'That might be whatever your dad has organised.
What else does it say?'

I went back to the screen. '"*A new man in your life.*"
Well, that can't be right. I don't want a new man in
my life. I'm happy with JJ.'

'Anything else?'

'Something about choice. The unexpected. And an encounter with someone from my past. Do you think that means Keira?"

'Maybe.'

'I was thinking about her on our way back here. I've done what she did by accident,' I said.

'Done what by accident?'

'Sprayed scent in the wrong direction. She was right, the nozzle is so small on those testers, it's hard to see sometimes and I've sprayed perfume right into my eyes by mistake before now.'

'So have I,' said Pia, 'but this is *Keira*. You're making excuses for her, Jess. I think she knew exactly what she was doing and where she was aiming. She knows that I'm not taken in by her. Never was, never will be. She's never liked me either.'

'Nor me,' I said.

'Jealous,' said Pia. 'She's always been jealous of you; she was even back in junior school.'

The front door opened and Charlie came in with Flo, Meg, Henry and Podge. Podge is a new mate of Charlie's and also in his band. God knows why his nickname is Podge because he's as thin as a rake. Flo and Meg are our mates from school – Flo is tall with big dreamy grey eyes and wavy blonde hair, Meg is small like Pia but that's where the likeness stops. Pia's style is colourful and girlie, Meg looks like a tomboy with her short hair and she lives in jeans and trainers. Flo and Charlie have been going out for a few months now and lately Meg has got together with Podge, which is nice because she was getting fed up with being the only singleton of the group. So now, all four of us are all loved up for the summer.

'Don't say anything about Keira,' I whispered. 'I don't want everyone getting into it.'

'Why not?' she asked. 'Everyone needs to know what a creep she is.'

'Who's a creep?' asked Flo.

'Needs to know what?' asked Charlie.

'Thanks,' I said to Pia. 'Nothing,' I said to Flo and Chaz.

'We bumped into Keira in Harrods,' Pia announced. 'She apologised to Jess for being a jerk at the modelling competition and then "accidentally" sprayed perfume tester in my face.'

'Yeah right,' said Meg. 'Accidentally on purpose, more like.'

Pia gave me a knowing look. 'Exactly.'

'Who's Keira?' asked Podge.

Charlie made his eyes cross, did a zombie stagger towards him and mock strangled him. 'She's the girl from your worst nightmare. She will scoop out your brain and eat it for breakfast. Yum, yum, slurp.'

'Let's talk about something else, shall we? She's taken up enough of our time already,' I said as the front door opened and Alisha, Alexei and JJ trooped in. As always, they looked glossy and effortlessly chic, like they'd stepped out of a *Vogue* magazine shoot. JJ and Alisha with their dark good lucks and Alexei in contrast with his floppy blond hair, pale skin and blue eyes. Alexei is Russian and lives in one of the upstairs apartments. He's an only child, home-schooled and like JJ and Alisha, was glad to find friends here in the UK of his own age when he moved into No 1.

'Who's taken up enough of your time?' asked Alisha. 'I hope you're not talking about me.'

'Course not,' said Pia. 'We were talking about Keira.'

'Wasn't she that nutjob who got thrown out of the modelling competition for stealing your dress?' JJ asked.

I nodded.

'She came up to the apartment, didn't she?' said

Alisha. 'She was so desperate to be in with us, but I could tell it was only because she thought we might be of some use to her. A typical hanger-on.'

'She tried to get off with JJ,' said Charlie.

'And Tom. Though even he saw through her in the end.' I sighed. 'Can we please not talk about her? Look, it's a lovely day. I'm here with my best mates. Why ruin it?'

I looked around at them as they all flopped down to sit where they could: Alisha, Alexei and Meg squashed on the sofa; Charlie, Podge and Flo on the giant bean bags; JJ leaning on the bar next to Pia. All my favourite people, all so different to look at. Charlie and Flo like a romantic pair from a Pre-Raphaelite painting. Henry handsome, sturdy, straight off the rugby pitch. Alexei beautiful and angelic-looking. Alisha and JJ black, American, so cool. Meg in her usual jeans, and Pia, who was wearing a coral and red crepe vintage nineteen fifties dress she found in Notting Hill market.

'So, everyone ready for the hols?' I asked.

Charlie glanced at Alexei and then at me. 'Actually, Jess, I have something to tell you. Alexei's invited me over to stay in the South of France with him.'

'And me,' said Henry.

'Iz for boys' time,' said Alexei.

'How long for?' I asked.

Charlie shrugged and looked at Alexei. 'As long as we want,' he said.

'But I thought that Dad had arranged something for us, Chaz?'

Charlie looked slightly uncomfortable. 'I checked with him. He said I can go to France with the boys.'

'So where am I going?' I asked.

Charlie's face flushed. 'Er . . . I'll let him tell you,' he said.

'Surprise?' asked Pia.

Charlie nodded then looked away. I guessed that he felt bad about not accompanying me to wherever the mystery destination was. I was still hoping it was going to be with the Lewis family to somewhere fabulous. I'd be fine on my own with them if that happened, especially now that I knew that Charlie would be having a fabulous time of his own.

'Is it OK with you that I go?' Henry asked Pia.

'Course,' said Pia. 'I'll be in Denmark for the first week, anyway. I'm really glad you're going.' I nodded that I agreed with her. After our amazing trip to India in the Easter holidays, I couldn't begrudge Charlie a brilliant holiday too. I'd felt guilty at the time that he had been left behind and I know that Pia felt the same about Henry. I was glad they'd be getting a treat themselves. I knew a trip to the South of France with Alexei wouldn't be dossing down in a tent anywhere. It probably meant travelling in a private plane, a chauffeur to pick them up in a limo and accommodation in some stunning location with the best of everything laid on. Sometimes it bothered me that I couldn't repay the treats that JJ, Alexei and Alisha gave us, although Pia is always reminding me that it's our friendship that means a lot to them, not presents or anything like that.

It's strange to think that the teen residents at Porchester Park seem to have it all – designer everything, extravagance all the way – but the one thing that money can't buy them is mates. All the same, I wished I could return some of their generosity. Like today, Alisha handed me a little bag with a pink ribbon when she arrived and inside were a dozen freshly baked fudge chip cookies from a local deli. She never arrived empty-handed when she came to mine and always brought something divine to eat or drink. On my pocket money, what could I take up to her? A packet of chocolate HobNobs? It just wasn't the same.

'A boys' holiday? Are you going, JJ?' I asked, suddenly worrying that my plans to spend time with him over the break might not happen after all.

'Er ... I have been invited but ...' He glanced at his sister. 'Actually, I need to talk to you, Jess. In private.'

'Oh, yes,' I said. 'I got your text.' Again the shiver of anticipation ran through me. I was sure that I was going to be invited to go on holiday with them. Charlie was going to go with Alexei and I was going to go with the Lewises. Yay. It was then that I noticed that Alisha was looking down. 'You OK, Alisha?' I asked. Her eyes filled with sudden tears which she tried to brush away.

I jumped off my stool. 'Come upstairs,' I said and led her up to my room before anyone else noticed. JJ followed after us. As soon as I closed the door behind the three of us, Alisha burst into tears.

'Hey, what is it?' I asked as I gave her a hug. I looked to JJ for explanation.

'It's Gramps,' he said. 'His heart.'

'Oh no,' I said as the penny dropped. 'That's what you had to tell me? Is he going to be OK?'

JJ nodded. 'We just heard this morning. He was rushed into hospital last night with heart failure and is in intensive care. We're flying to the States tonight.'

'*Tonight?*' I blurted.

'He couldn't even come on Skype,' said Alisha, 'and he always does that.'

'Alisha's very close to him,' said JJ, and this time *his* eyes filled with tears. 'We're all very close to him. He virtually brought us up in the beginning when Dad was just starting out as an actor and away a lot.'

'God, I'm so sorry. How awful for you all. Is he your mum's father or your dad's?'

'Dad's,' said JJ.

'So how's your dad doing?'

JJ shook his head. 'I've never seen my dad so upset. He just wants to make sure he gets there in …' JJ could hardly say the words.

'I understand.'

JJ took my hand. 'I know we had so many things planned for the summer, Jess, but everything is up in the air now for all of us. For instance, one of Mum's friends from the States had planned to stay with us over the holiday. She only arrived yesterday, and now she's going to be in the apartment on her own. Mum feels so bad about leaving her, but we have no choice. We don't know how long we'll be gone or when we'll be back.'

I felt my heart sink as my dreams of a summer with JJ faded, but I told myself not to be selfish. This wasn't the time to be thinking about my feelings. 'When are you leaving? Tonight, you said?'

He nodded. 'Mum's packing now.'

'I wish there was something I could do,' I said.

'I wish there was something *anybody* could do,' said JJ. 'He's got the best possible care, best doctors in the world but even they can't always work miracles.'

I glanced over at Alisha. I had never seen her so quiet. I went and put my arm around her. 'I guess this means all your plans are out of the window too.'

She nodded. Just as I'd had plans to hang out with JJ, Alisha had plans to spend time with her boyfriend Prasad. She'd met him in India in the Easter holidays and they'd got on immediately. Luckily, he went to school here in England so they'd managed to see each other some weekends, but not for long and rarely without a minder being present. I knew Alisha was looking forward to some time alone with Prasad before he flew back to his parents' hotel in Rajastan. 'Does Prasad know?'

'I told him this morning, straight after we'd got the news,' Alisha replied. 'He understood that we have to put Gramps first.'

I nodded. I knew only too well from my own experiences with my mum how it felt to see a loved one suffer and feel utterly helpless. Suddenly Keira and her nastiness was the last of my concerns. One of my best mates and my boyfriend were going through a hellish time.

After they'd gone back up to their apartment, I stared out of my window and realised that my summer hopes and dreams were changing fast. No five-star luxury in the Caribbean or white-beached island for me, not even hanging about in London with JJ. The boys were all going away to Europe, Pia would be off to Denmark, Flo was going up to Scotland and Meg to Cornwall. It suddenly dawned on me that I was going to be all by myself. *Not that it matters*, I thought as I remembered Alisha's sad face and wished there was something I could do to make her feel better.

I picked up Dave to have a cuddle. 'At least I have you,' I said as I stroked his furry head. 'You haven't abandoned me.'

He wasn't in the mood though, and jumped down from my lap. Like all cats, cuddles happen when they want it, not when their human does. He put his nose in the air and left the room. 'Huh. Fickle cat,' I called after him. 'I'm always your friend when you want feeding.'

I sighed, opened my notebook and wrote.

July. Random thoughts on happiness:
Knowing that loved ones are well and happy.
Sinking your teeth into a freshly baked cookie.
Spending time with best of friends.
Cuddling my cat (when he's in the mood).

3

Goodbye and Hello

'I promise I'll Skype every day,' said JJ. 'And text and email.'

I put my arms around his neck and leant up to kiss him. He kissed me back and we stayed for a few moments with our arms around each other. We were in the sitting room of the Lewises' apartment, a couple of hours after he'd told me about his grandfather. Over his shoulder, I could see a stunning pink and gold dusk sky through the floor-to-ceiling windows that looked out over Hyde Park. Like all the windows in the apartment block, we could see out but no-one could see in. The glass was also bullet-proof.

The security at the block had been designed by the SAS so that the apartments were super safe with all the latest technology. The sky was so beautiful and being in JJ's arms felt so good, it would have been the perfect romantic moment if I hadn't known that he and his family would be leaving within the hour.

We held on to each other and I knew he was feeling the same sadness that I was. As we stood there, I remembered the first time I'd seen JJ in the spa area, and later how shy I'd been when we finally got to talk at Alisha's fifteenth birthday party, never imagining for a moment that a boy like him would be interested in someone like me – especially as I was dressed up as a monster at the time!

I'd worried that we wouldn't last as a couple because I wasn't from his world, but it had never been a problem between us and we had become very close, particularly in the last few weeks when I'd been finishing off exams. He'd been really supportive and understanding if I'd needed to study and couldn't see him. Even though we'd only been together a short while, we still had many special memories. We often seemed to be laughing together, like the day we escaped from his minder and took shelter from the rain under two huge umbrellas in Hyde Park, just so we could be alone. And we'd tried hard to show each other our lives – me going away with him on a private plane to India and staying in a seven-star hotel when we got there, and him hanging out in the chill-out shed at the bottom of our garden where Charlie and I liked to go with mates after school.

I'd listened to JJ talk about his plans for his future at university and I'd spoken to him about my indecision about what I wanted to do when I left school; he was so sure of his plans and wanted to put something back into the world, I still had no idea of where I was going to fit. Whatever we talked about and wherever we were, I loved hanging out with him and was going to miss him a lot.

Finally JJ let me go. 'Seeing you on Skype just won't be the same as this. You can't do cyber kisses or smell someone's perfume or the apple scent from their shampoo.'

I smiled. 'We should get an IT man onto it immediately,' I said. I was trying to be as cheerful as I could be, even though inside I felt like crying. Neither of us knew when we'd be together again and I didn't want him to remember me being sad.

'JJ honey,' called Mrs Lewis from the hall. 'You almost done?'

'All packed, Mom,' JJ called back. 'They can take my bags down.'

Alisha came in and straight over to us. She put her arms around us both. 'Group hug,' she said. 'I'm going to miss you so much, Jess.'

'Me too,' I said. 'We can Skype.'

'Seriously, we must,' said Alisha. 'As often as we can.'

'OK, car's here, guys,' called Mrs Lewis.

'I'm going to go,' I said. I gave them a last squeeze each. I wasn't going to go down to the car with them in case I blubbed. JJ nodded. He understood. I glanced at Alisha. Her eyes were full of tears.

'Hey, it isn't forever,' I said. 'I'll see you again.'

'I know, I just don't know when,' she said, then gave me another hug. 'God, I hate goodbyes. Like, total emotion overload.'

I laughed. 'Yeah and crying can *ruin* your make-up.'

That made Alisha laugh. With a last look at JJ, I made myself leave.

Once I was in the lift, a sob rose from deep in my chest and at last, I let the tears I'd been holding back come to the surface. *The hard thing about having a boyfriend you really like*, I thought, *is when you have to be separated*. I sniffed back the tears. I knew that there were cameras in every part of Porchester Park, lifts included. I didn't want any of the security men to see me crying and ask why. I took a deep breath. I would save my tears until I was alone in my bedroom and I could cry without worrying who was watching.

In the meantime, I need cheering up, I told myself. I decided to go straight to Dad and ask him where he'd organised for me to go on my break. I needed a change of scenery, away from Porchester Park and the empty space that JJ would leave here. *Hearing about my surprise holiday and having something to look forward to*, I thought, *that should help*.

As the lift doors opened on the ground floor to let me out, I saw that a lady was waiting to get in. I recognised her immediately this time. It was Stephanie Harper.

She looked at me for a moment. 'Say, haven't we met?'

I nodded. 'This morning in Harrods. I handed your case back to you.'

'Oh, right. Of course. You live here?'

I pointed upstairs. 'Just visiting friends. Saying goodbye, actually. They're going back to the States.'

'Not the Lewis family?'

I nodded.

'No kidding? What a coincidence. I'm staying in their apartment while they're away.'

'You're Mrs Lewis's friend?'

Ms Harper nodded.

'JJ told me that someone was staying there while they're away,' I said.

'Yep. It's me. So if you're visiting here, where do you actually live?'

I pointed to the staff area. 'My dad's the general manager. We have a house back there.'

'Mr Hall?' She smiled. 'He's a Capricorn, right?'

'Yes. His birthday is at the beginning of January.'

'A workaholic?'

I nodded. Ms Harper looked at me closely, like she was looking right into me. 'And you're Sagittarian, yes?'

I nodded. 'How did you know?'

'It's my business to. I'm an astrologer so I can usually guess what signs people are.' She was still looking at me and I got the feeling that she knew I'd been crying. 'It's going to be a rough few days for Sagittarians. Rough for a lot of signs, actually. Plans going out the window. It's due to the influence of Uranus, that's the planet of the unexpected. It's in a difficult position right now. Square to Pluto. Try and ride the changes, hon. What you resist, persists.' She looked at her watch. 'Hey, I'd better get up there if I'm going to catch them before they leave. I'm sure I'll see you around and we'll talk some more, OK?' She stepped into the lift, the doors shut and she was gone.

'Love to,' I said.

4

A Trip Away

'Bournemouth,' said Dad, after I'd found him in his office.

'*Bournemouth?*' I gasped. I knew I sounded disappointed but I couldn't help it. I *was* disappointed.

'Yes, to stay with your aunt and uncle for a couple of weeks. What were you expecting?'

I slumped down in the chair opposite his desk. 'I don't know. Er . . . maybe somewhere a bit more special.'

Dad sighed.

'What's the matter, Dad?'

Dad hesitated for a moment, then sighed again.

'This is, Jess,' he finally said. 'A year or so ago, you'd have been jumping up and down about a week in Bournemouth and the chance to be at the coast in July but … your reaction, see, that's exactly why I want you to go.'

'What do you mean?'

Dad indicated upstairs. 'I wonder whether mixing with the residents since you moved here, with the Lewises, Tanisha, Alexei, I wonder if it hasn't spoilt you a little – raised your expectations to the point that you're disappointed to be going to spend time with my brother and his family and not flying off to some exotic luxury resort with A-listers. You've begun to want a lifestyle that I can't afford and, frankly, neither will you when you're older, unless you win the Eurolottery.'

'So let's go and buy a ticket,' I said.

Dad didn't laugh and I could see that he was upset. 'I want the best for you, Jess, you know I do, but you have to learn that the best of life and true happiness doesn't always come with a five-star rating, a designer label or price tag.'

'I know that, Dad, I'm not totally stupid. But … Charlie's going to stay with Alexei so he'll be staying in all the best places, and in Bournemouth, Uncle

John and Aunt Cissie don't even have a proper room for me. I'll have to sleep on the sofabed in the sitting room.'

Dad nodded. 'Nothing wrong with that. And you know it was Charlie's turn for a treat after your Indian trip.'

'I do and I'm glad he'll be going.'

Dad stared out of the window. He looked tired, as he often did these days, and I noticed that there was more silver appearing in his dark hair. His job as general manager meant he was on call twenty-four hours a day. I can't remember the last time he had a weekend or even a whole day off. If he tried to take a few hours, there was always someone calling his iPhone, some crisis to sort out. He'd probably have loved a few days in Bournemouth with his brother. He was also right – hanging out with the Lewises had shown me another side of life, a side I'd come to like.

'I don't know, Jess,' Dad said. 'I wonder if I did the wrong thing bringing you and Charlie to live in this place, to put the lifestyle of the residents right under your noses. I don't want you to ever feel that you've missed out but … you know these people are the exception.'

'Dad, I'm fine. I'm not feeling bitter or envious or

anything like that. Honestly. I'm glad I've been able to have a taste of how the other half live, a glimpse of that world.' I suddenly thought of Alisha's stricken face and JJ's sad eyes before they left for the States. 'Believe me, I know that although it's all very nice, there are still some things money can't buy – like good health and good mates.'

'That's certainly true.' Dad turned back to look at me and smiled. 'When did you get so wise?'

I shrugged. 'Not wise. I just see what's going on around me. JJ and Alisha are so sad about their grand-father.'

'I know. I heard their news this afternoon and I'm aware that you'll miss them, Jess. I know you've had it tough in many respects, moving here, so much change at such a young age ...' I knew he was refer-ring to Mum's death. He rarely spoke about her any more. I'd learnt that his way of dealing with anything painful was to keep busy and not give in to being emotional. 'I really do want what's best for you, you know.'

I decided to put away my disappointment. Dad didn't need it on top of everything else he had to deal with. His job was full time, like now, still working on a Saturday night when most people are at home relaxing or off out somewhere. 'I know, Dad,' I said. 'And Bournemouth will be fine, fab in fact. Wasn't Mum always saying life is what you make it? The choices you make. I choose to have a good time there. I'll make the best of it, sofabed and all. OK?'

'OK,' said Dad. 'And while we're having this chat, there's another thing. When you get back, I'd like you to look for some holiday work. I'll even see if I can find you something to do around Porchester Park.'

'Work?'

Dad nodded. 'Yes, work. I want you to learn that money doesn't always come so easily as it does for some of the residents of Porchester Park.'

'I *do* know that. I *really* know that. And actually, the Lewis family weren't always rich and now Mr Lewis works very hard for his wealth. JJ told me that his dad often says that fame is fickle and one day he might be at the top, but the next, he could be yesterday's news. So I *do* know money doesn't grow on trees and all that.'

'Do you, Jess? I wonder if you've lost sight a bit.'

'Well, I can tell you I haven't,' I snapped. I felt cross that he could say such a thing. Lose sight that money didn't come easily? Hah. I'd never been more aware of it. Dad had no idea how hard it was sometimes, like going shopping with Alisha and seeing her spend in five minutes more than I'd get in pocket money in twenty years. Letting her always pick up the bill because she knew that I couldn't afford to. Not feeling I could pay my own way when we were out. I didn't say anything though because I didn't want Dad to see that it upset me in case he forbade me to go out with the Lewises in the future. 'OK, a job. Fine. But what will I do?'

'We'll work something out. Actually, I've been talking to Pia's mum about it. She agrees that Pia ought to do some work during the holidays too. In the meantime, your Uncle John has some jobs for you down in Bournemouth.'

'Jobs? In Bournemouth? You mean it's not even a break?'

'Only babysitting and I'm sure he'll give you some time off. He and Cissie want to repaint the house but can't do it with the two boys around. He asked if you might be free to look after them, take them out the way so that they can get on.'

The news was getting worse and worse. Any mental images I'd had of sitting on a sun lounger in Tuscany, being waited on by some gorgeous Italian boy, or sitting on a beach in St Ives licking a Cornish ice cream were disappearing fast. *Babysitting in Bournemouth? I don't believe it!* I was about to object when Dad's phone rang.

'One day, we'll go somewhere truly fab. Just the three of us. You, me and Charlie,' he said before he took the call.

'Sure,' I said. *And pigs might fly*, I thought. *With Dad's commitments here, that's not going to happen until I'm an old lady with a zimmer frame.*

As Dad left the room with his phone glued to his ear, I went home to call Gran. I was sure she would sympathise and put Dad straight about the fact that I needed a holiday. Her and Aunt Maddie were brilliant at Easter when the Lewises invited me to India and, at first, Dad wouldn't let me go because he knew I had a lot of studying to do. They were round in a flash telling him it was a fantastic experience and I shouldn't miss out. He couldn't argue against the dynamic duo. I just needed them to do the same this time.

'I think that's wonderful, darling,' said Gran, after I'd got through and blurted out the latest to her. 'I think your dad's right. It's a wonderful lesson to learn the value of earning your own money.'

'Wh … whaaaat?' I stuttered. Her response was not what I expected … She so didn't understand. I *got* the value of earning your own money, I just didn't want to do it yet. *Shall I speak to Aunt Maddie?* I asked myself when I finished my call with Gran. No point. I knew in my gut exactly what her view would be – same as Dad's and Gran's, in fact she'd probably have a list of jobs for me to try.

What would Mum have had to say? I wondered. I often tried to imagine her opinion on something or what her answer to a question would be. I made myself still so I could tune in. As I settled, I could almost hear her voice … 'All good experience.' Bummer. She was with the others. 'OK, Mum,' I said. 'I hear you.'

I called Pia.

'I've heard,' she said as soon as she answered the phone.

'Isn't it awful? Did your mum tell you what kind of jobs we'll be doing when I get back?'

'Yep. Apparently Henry's dad has said we can help out washing the cars in the garages while Henry is away and Mum always needs help cleaning in the spa too. She said there's loads of other stuff we can do around the apartment block too.'

My heart sank. 'Whoopeedoop. At Easter, with the

invite to join the Lewis family in India, it was a case of Cinderella, you shall go to the ball. This holiday, it's a case of Cinderella, you *shan't* go to the ball. Now get in the kitchen, get the rubber gloves on and get scrubbing.'

'I know. Oh, how the mighty are fallen,' said Pia then she laughed. 'It'll be OK, Jess. If we're in it together, it'll be a laugh.'

Thank God for friends, I thought after I'd hung up. *Thank God for Pia.*

<u>Who am I?</u>
A slave to my family.

<u>Who or what do I want to be?</u>
Independent and very, very rich,
whilst at the same time totally
understanding that money cannot
buy you true happiness.
(I do know that despite what Dad says but being rich can sure let you off doing the chores!)

<u>Happiness is:</u>
A pal like Pia to do the chores with.

5

A Boy and His Dog

It was raining when I set off for Waterloo station a few days later. As a treat, Dad asked Henry's dad, Mr Sawtell, to give me a lift to the station in one of the apartments' Mercedes. He was going in the direction of the station so was happy to do so.

After he'd dropped me off, I headed across the marble concourse, which was slippy from the many travellers with dripping umbrellas who rushed across it, heading for platforms and their trains. I joined the long queue snaking its way towards the ticket office and as I glanced at the people in the line, a boy in front of me caught my eye. I noticed him because he was talking to his dog, an Irish terrier, who was listening with rapt attention.

When he turned around and I saw his face, I felt my cheeks redden so I quickly turned away in case he saw my reaction. Drop. Dead. Gorgeous. He was tall and slim, with tousled brown hair and a tanned, open face. He was also clearly an animal lover, which is always a big plus in my book. Dave, my cat, is one of my best friends and I often talk to him in the same way that the boy in the queue was talking to his dog.

The queue moved forward, the boy bought his ticket and moved off to catch his train, his dog trotting along by his side. As I watched him go, I wondered where he was going and where he'd come from. He was dressed in a pair of old jeans and a checked shirt and had a look of the open air about him, like he lived by the ocean or led an outdoors life, unlike so many English boys who were white and pasty after a long winter and cold spring.

Once I'd got my ticket, I glanced at the departure board and saw that a train was leaving in eight minutes so I pelted across the concourse, through the ticket barrier and jumped on to the nearest carriage. The train was almost full so I sat in the nearest seat or rather fell because the train lurched as it began to pull out of the station.

'Hope you don't mind dogs,' said a male voice with a slight Australian accent.

'Oh, it's you!' I said when I saw that I had sat down next to the boy from the queue. His dog put his paw up on my knee as if to say hi.

'Me? Have we met?' he asked.

'Um ... No, I saw you in the ticket queue. Er ... I don't mind dogs. I like them,' I said. 'As long as he doesn't bite.'

'He doesn't,' said the boy, then he smiled. 'I do though.'

His eyes were the colour of dark honey. *Trouble*, my mind told me. *He's far too good-looking not to be.*

'Vampire or do you have behavioural problems?' I asked.

'Depends on who I'm with,' said the boy, then he laughed and shook his head. 'Sorry. I'm not usually like this. Um. Start again, shall I? Hi. I'm Connor and this is my dog, Raffy.'

I took the dog's paw. 'Hi Raffy,' I said. 'I think you need to keep your owner under control. He's clearly not safe out without a lead.'

'And you are?'

'Oh, yes, I'm perfectly safe without a lead.'

Connor cracked up. 'No, I didn't mean that. I meant and you are, as in, who are you?'

'I knew that,' I said. *There is major flirting going on here!* I thought. 'Jess. Jess Hall. Animal lover. I don't bite and I have a cat called Dave.'

'Dave?'

'Dave. I like to talk to him too. I saw you were talking to Raffy in the queue, that's why I noticed you. My friends think I'm mad, but I know he gets the meaning behind what I'm saying.'

Connor nodded. 'Exactly.'

I got out my book to signal that although friendly, I was not necessarily available. I had a boyfriend even if he was going away for a while, plus I like to be quiet on train journeys, to read or stare out of the window and reflect on things. And I had a lot to reflect on. It felt like my whole life had been turned upside down in the last few days with all my plans for the summer disappearing like water down a plug-hole.

Connor got the message. He turned away and stared out of the window too and Raffy settled down by his feet and went to sleep. After a while, Connor pulled a book out of the rucksack which was in front of him. I glanced at it to see what he was reading.

Mum always said that people's books reveal a lot about them – books and their shoes. I'd already clocked that Connor was wearing a battered pair of blue Converse Allstars. I was wearing my favourite red pair.

'Hey! Snap,' I said and showed Connor my book. We were both reading *One Day* by David Nicholls, a book about a couple who meet at university then the story catches up with them on the same day every year as they get older.

Connor laughed and put down his book. 'Enjoying it?'

I shrugged. 'Yes. My gran gave it to me for the journey. She's always giving me stuff to read. I wouldn't have thought it was a boy's book, though.'

'It's not my usual kind of thing but it's not bad. Someone had left it on the Tube on my way to the station so I picked it up.'

'Do you think it's possible to have only one true love of your life like in the book?' I asked.

Connor nodded. 'And I've met mine.' *Oh*, I thought, *flirting over*. I felt disappointed even though I knew it couldn't go anywhere because I was in a relationship with JJ. Connor looked down at his dog. 'Raffy. He is the true love of my life. He gets me completely. He loves me unconditionally and never complains.'

I laughed. 'Me too with Dave. He is the love of my life for ever and always.'

Connor smiled as if he liked my answer. 'So. Where you are heading?'

'Bournemouth. You?'

'Same. You live there?'

I shook my head. 'Visiting family. You?' I was beginning to sound like a record that had got stuck. *You? You? Think of something else to say*, I told myself.

'Visiting my sister. She's just moved there. Where do you live?' Connor replied.

'London. Knightsbridge.'

'Posh.'

'Very. That's me. Me and the Queen. We're very posh. Where do you live? I detect an Australian accent, don't I?'

Connor nodded. 'I grew up in Sydney, but I've come over to study here so now I live in North London. Highgate. Medium posh. Whereabouts in Knightsbridge, Jess?'

I suddenly found I wanted to impress him. 'No 1, Porchester Park. It's an apartment block.'

Connor shook his head. 'Can't say I know it.

You're right in the heart of things down there though, hey?'

'Yeah. It's handy for Harrods.'

'I know Harrods and the Victoria and Albert museum and that's about it. I prefer the countryside myself,' said Connor. 'So does Raffy.'

'What are you going to study?'

'I've started already. Just done my first year in photography.'

'Good course?' I asked.

'Very,' said Connor.

I went back to reading my book for a while and so did Connor. I liked that. He wasn't pushy.

After about half an hour, my phone bleeped that I had a text.

It was from Pia. Have u seen ur facebk pge 2day?

I texted back. No. Why?

Nothing. Call me l8r.

I texted back. Has JJ left a msge?

No. I'll talk 2 U l8r, Pia replied. Call me asap when U have Internet access.

She had me intrigued now. JJ had texted me before I left home and we'd Skyped last night, so who else could it be? I so wished that Dad would let me have a phone with Internet access instead of the ancient model I have, but he said we can't afford it at the moment

I texted back. What is it?

This time she didn't reply, so there was nothing I could do but forget about it, although I had a horrible niggling feeling in the pit of my stomach. I went back to my reading.

As we got close to Bournemouth, Connor finally closed his book.

'You here for long?' he asked.

'Just a couple of weeks.' For a moment, I felt torn. I was sure he was about to ask for my number, but I had a boyfriend, didn't I? What should I say? I got up to let him and Raffy out. He slung his rucksack over his shoulder and we both went to stand in the corridor ready to get off. I wondered if it would be OK to give him my number as long as we stayed just friends? He was very attractive, looked interesting and would make my visit to Bournemouth more fun. *Who are you kidding?* I asked myself. No way would I want to be friends with a boy like Connor. I could feel major chemistry between us as we stood close waiting for the train to pull in and I was sure he could feel it too. It was like heat pulling me towards him and I was having to resist not reaching up to touch his face. *Stop this right now, Jess Hall*, I told myself. *I have a boyfriend, a lovely boyfriend. He hasn't even been gone a few days and I shouldn't already be looking at other boys!*

As the train finally drew into the station, stopped and the doors opened, Connor turned back to me.

'Nice meeting you, Jess. Have a good stay,' he said, then off he went. No date, no number, no nothing. My inner conflict was a total waste of time.

I felt disappointed as I watched him walk away, rejected even, but maybe it was for the best, I told myself. There was still JJ to think of – but all the same, no harm in appreciating beauty and I liked to think I still had some pulling power. Maybe Connor was gay? Or maybe I just wasn't his type. *Maybe he's already got a girlfriend somewhere*, I told myself as I made my way along the platform. *Or maybe I'm too young, too pasty-faced? Maybe he prefers outdoor-type girls with sunkissed hair and tanned legs?*

Luckily I didn't have too long to mull it over because I could see Uncle John waving and smiling at the end of the platform.

6

Family Time

'So how's your dad?' asked Aunt Cissie as she put eggs, peppers and herbs out onto the kitchen counter. My six-year-old cousin, Louis, was standing on a stool next to her dressed in a red-and-white chef's hat and apron.

'Fine. He works too hard,' I said as I watched Louis break eggs into a bowl.

'And you like it there at that fancy apartment block?' asked Uncle John as he sat at the pine kitchen table and pushed his hair out of his eyes. He's dad's younger brother and although dark-haired and blue-eyed like Dad, the similarity stops there. Dad's dress sense is executive and immaculate in his smart work suits. Uncle John, who's a maths teacher, always looks dishevelled, lives in jeans and T-shirts and is often known to wear odd socks with his battered old sneakers. Auntie Cissie, who's a French teacher, lives in jeans as well and with her long ginger hair has the look of an old hippie. Neither of them have ever seemed bothered about the latest fashions or designer wear.

I nodded. 'It's different.'

'Different how?' he asked.

'You get two very different worlds on the same site. The staff area and the residents' area. The staff are pretty normal and our mews houses ordinary, nice, but nothing posh whereas the apartments where the rich residents live are out of this world, like some of their kitchens are the size of the whole of the ground floor of this house. I've seen inside some of them and they're awesome. One resident had the whole of a sixteenth century chateau transported over and incorporated into their apartment. And they don't have posters on the wall, they have the originals, like Picasso or Rembrandt or Monet. Others go for everything brand new but it's all the best in the whole world, marble floors from Italy or France, living rooms as big as football fields. So different in that sort of way.'

Aunt Cissie laughed. 'It's different here too. I'm sorry not to have a proper room and bed to offer you. I'd put you in with the boys but Louis sometimes gets up in the night still and would wake you.'

'I'm Master Chef tonight,' Louis told me as he began to chop peppers under the close scrutiny of his mother. 'You hungry?'

'Starving,' I replied.

'Good. We're having Spanish omelette.'

'My favourite,' I said. 'What's your favourite?'

'Custard,' he replied.

Now I had arrived, I found that I didn't mind sleeping in the living room at all. I liked the comfy, family feel of their home, with toys, DVDs, CDs and books scattered everywhere. It felt lived in, as opposed to the immaculate rooms and corridors at No 1, Porchester Park, or at home some evenings when Dad was working and Charlie was out and our house felt so quiet. I'd always got on with Uncle John and Aunt Cissie and their two boys were sweet. Sam was nine years old and quietly thoughtful while Louis was full of energy and chatter.

'Just let us know if there's anything you need,' said Uncle John.

'Have you got a computer I could take a quick look

at?' I asked. Pia had texted again that I should look at my Facebook page.

Uncle John pointed upstairs. 'In my study. Come up.'

He led me up to a cramped office, the size of a broom cupboard, took some papers off the seat at his desk and indicated I should sit down. 'Piles of lesson plans for next term,' he said. 'You thought about what you want to do when you leave school yet?'

I shook my head. 'I keep changing my mind. Got to get my GCSE results first before I make any decisions like that.'

'That's August, isn't it?'

I nodded.

'Confident?' asked Uncle John.

'Ish. I did study hard for them but won't relax completely until I know I've done OK.'

'I'm sure you will, Jess.'

'I hope so. When the results are in, I'll think seriously about what I want to do at university.'

'Don't worry too much. Students often change course mid-term. You know how to use an Apple Mac?'

I nodded. 'We use a Mac at home.'

'OK, just shout if you need anything.'

'Thanks,' I said as Uncle John left the room.

I quickly logged in to my Facebook page and scanned the screen for messages. A shiver went through me as I read the new message on my wall. Someone had posted a link to an *I hate Jess Hall* page.

I felt myself go cold as I clicked through to the page. There was a photo of me when I was younger, about nine years old – a truly awful photo of me in the back garden of the house we lived in when Mum was alive. The picture had caught me at a bad angle, as though taken from below. I was pulling a face that made me look really snooty. Only one person could have had it apart from Pia or my family and I knew it would never be one of them. Keira. She'd lived on the same street and we used to hang out sometimes. Under the photo was written, *Click like if you agree that Jess Hall is a stuck-up cow*. Three people had clicked.

I felt a sinking feeling in my stomach. *Please don't say Kiera's out to get me again*, I thought. As well as attempting to ruin my chances in the modelling competition earlier in the year, Keira had sent me some nasty emails. They had really upset me but they stopped after the competition and because I hadn't heard from her for ages, I'd hoped that she'd lost interest in her vendetta against me and moved on.

I went back to my page and quickly deleted the link from my wall then texted Pia: Seen it.

A few moments later, my mobile rang. 'You OK?' Pia asked.

'Yes. No. I've deleted the link but I bet loads of people have seen it already. It has to be Keira, doesn't it? No-one else could have got hold of that photo. I really hope this isn't the start of something again.'

'You could report Keira to Facebook. They can remove the page she's put up and chances are she'll be banned.'

'Why me, Pia? Why's she targeting me again?'

'I told you last time. She's jealous.'

'But why? She's got nothing to be jealous of.'

'Is everything OK, Jess?' asked Aunt Cissie. I hadn't heard her come in behind me.

'I ... yes, fine,' I said.

'I've got to go anyway, Jess,' said Pia. 'Speak later and don't stress, OK?'

I quickly left the Facebook page so that Aunt Cissie wouldn't see it.

'Something up?' she asked.

I shook my head. I didn't want to talk about it and if I didn't react, hopefully Keira would go away and it wouldn't amount to anything.

'Come on down then if you've finished up here. Master Chef Louis's omelette is ready.'

I got up to follow her but eating was the last thing I felt like. I'd lost my appetite completely.

Happiness is:
Sitting on a train staring out the window as the world flashes by outside.
A sweet dog giving me his paw and saying hello.
A cute boy with honey-coloured eyes flirting.

Unhappiness is:
Feeling that someone out there doesn't like me and is thinking bad things about me.

7

Nanny McMe

'Have you never heard of the term "lie in"?' I asked Louis the next morning when he bounced onto the end of my bed at seven in the morning.

'It's the holidays,' he said. 'That means things to do.'

'Not always,' I said. 'Sometimes it means lying about doing nothing.' I snuggled back into my pillow. 'Or extra sleeping.'

He picked up a cushion from the floor and biffed me over the head with it. 'Come on, Jess. Time for breakfast.'

'Remind me never to have children,' I said as Uncle John's blurry face appeared around the door.

He sighed. 'Too late for me. If only I'd known. Come on, Louis, leave Jess alone to get up.'

The next few days were a whirlwind of activity. Up at seven. Feed the boys. Coco Pops for Sam. Fruit for Louis but 'only pears and they have to be cut up'. Sort the boys' clothes out. T-shirt and jeans for Sam. Has to be blue for Louis and he insists on wearing his Spider-Man outfit on top. Then on with my job, which was to take them out of the house so Uncle John and Aunt Cissie could get on with their painting, so it was out to the beach, play football, tennis, cricket, rounders – anything to keep them occupied. I hoped I'd maybe bump into Connor while we were out but there was no sign of him anywhere.

In the evening, I'd tuck the boys up on the sofa, one under each of my arms, to watch CBBC. I liked our TV time when they were tired and snuggly and smelt of soap after their baths.

It all went smoothly apart from the fourth afternoon after we'd been watching a repeat of *Doctor Who* on the television. I was washing up in the kitchen when Louis came up behind me.

'I'd like to be a Dalek instead of Spider-Man now,' he said. 'I need a costume.'

'OK,' I said and searched around for anything to help make him a costume. At first, I thought about maybe using some tinfoil to give him the metallic robot look, then I spied the sink plunger on the window sill behind the sink. *Perfect*, I thought. I picked it up, rinsed it under the tap and gave it to Louis. 'Here,' I said, 'stick that to your forehead and you'll look just like a Dalek.'

'Brilliant,' said Louis. He took the plunger and put it up to his forehead. The suction from the rubber worked perfectly and Louis ran off to show Sam his DIY raygun appendage. I finished the dishes and went through to the living room where Louis was trying to remove the sink plunger from his head.

'It won't come off,' he wailed.

'Course it will,' I said and went over to him. I pulled on the plunger, but the more I tugged, the stronger the suction on his skin, and I could see that he was beginning to get distressed. Uncle John and Aunt Cissie had gone out for painting supplies but they had been gone almost an hour and would be back any minute. It wouldn't look good to get back to find that their youngest son was freaking out because the babysitter had stuck a sink plunger to his head.

I pulled again.

'Ow,' Louis objected as Sam joined in the pulling. We tried everything – getting him to relax, lie on his side, gently trying to prise it off, but nothing was working; the plunger was glued solid to his skin and his mouth was beginning to wobble as if he was fighting back tears.

'Will I have to go out looking like this?' he asked.

'Well, you can pretend you're an alien,' I said. 'Everyone will think that you're so cool.'

He didn't look convinced.

'Mum and Dad,' said Sam as we heard the sound of their car pulling into the driveway.

'Oh God, they're going to kill me,' I said. 'Sam. Create a diversion.'

'Right,' he said. 'Um. What?'

I suddenly remembered a trick that Charlie played on Mum one April Fool's Day when we were little. 'Tomato ketchup. Squirt some on your head and lie at the bottom of the stairs in the hall.'

'Right,' said Sam. 'Brilliant.'

This only upset Louis more. 'I want to do that,' he said.

'You can tomorrow,' I promised.

I found the ketchup and handed it to Sam who

went out into the hall while I continued my search for something to help release the sink plunger. I noticed a bottle of olive oil next to the cooker.

'Oil!' I said. 'That should act as a lubricant. Yes. That will do it.'

Louis glanced at me coming towards him with the olive oil. 'I'm not a potato,' he said, then glanced out into the hall at his brother who had liberally applied the red gooey liquid to his head and was lying on the floor moaning.

'You're not like other babysitters, are you?' he asked as I got busy applying olive oil around his forehead where the plunger was attached.

'Probably not,' I said as the oil oozed under the rubber and the plunger began to slide a little. With a gentle tug, I heard a *thwuck* sound and the plunger finally came off and we both fell back.

Oh no, I thought as I reached out to catch Louis. It had left a perfect bright red circle where it had been stuck to his forehead.

A scream from the hall distracted us as Aunt Cissie came in the front door to find Sam lying at the foot of the stairs, looking like he was covered in blood.

'Oh my God!' cried Uncle John, who came in behind her and ran over to Sam.

'April Fool!' cried Sam and sprang up.

"April Fool?' asked Aunt Cissie. Neither she or Uncle John seemed to get the joke. They both looked well freaked out.

'It's July not April,' said Uncle John. 'You almost gave us a heart attack, Sam. Whose mad idea was this?'

Sam pointed at me. 'Jess's. And she got the sink plunger stuck on Louis's head.'

By this time, Louis had come into the hall and was looking at himself in the mirror. His parents noticed the mark on his forehead.

Uncle John turned to me. 'Jess?'

'He wanted to be a Dalek. Er, yes ... You have to be creative with boys, don't you?' I reached behind me and picked up a pan. 'Anyone want to try the pan on the head trick? Maybe not. Charlie tried it when he was younger. We had to call out the fire brigade when it got completely stuck. Um. Right. Thanks a lot. I'm going to go up to my bedroom now. Oh. I haven't got one. Right. OK. Maybe I'll just go and hide under the table. Bye.'

The whole family stood in a line looking at me as if I was insane.

*

Once the boys were in bed that night, I had supper with Uncle John and Aunt Cissie. They'd recovered from their shock by then and were even laughing about the incidents so that was a relief. Later, I fell into my make-do bed exhausted and grateful that the past days had been so busy that it had taken my mind off the fact that JJ had gone and Keira had set up the Facebook page. It took a lot of willpower but I made myself stay away from the computer in the little spare time that I had. I knew I'd obsess if there were more posts on Keira's *I hate Jess* page.

Plus it was weird being down in Bournemouth, like I'd fallen into a parallel universe. Porchester Park, London and all that went with it, including Keira, seemed so far away. I thought about sending a message to Keira threatening to report her to Facebook, but being away from home, it didn't seem real, like a bad dream and not really part of my life. Maybe I was in some sort of denial but the days were going so fast and part of me wanted to pretend that Keira didn't exist and her comments on Facebook hadn't happened. I just hoped that my four hundred Facebook friends had been as busy as I had and hadn't seen her horrible link before I'd removed it. Pia was always telling me to take people who I don't know off my friends list and I had meant to but, like so many things, had never got around to it.

On the Monday morning, it was a gloriously sunny day so I filled a paddling pool in the back garden and as the boys played in it, I checked my mobile for messages.

There were three.

Skype me soon. Miss U. Gramps not so gd. JJ X

From Pia: I messged Keira 2 tell her 2 remove the page off Facebook or I'd report her. Result. It's gone. She's still got her own page though so I left a message on her wall saying she's a coward. XX.

Thank God for that, I thought as I clicked on to the last message.

Too soon. It was from Keira. She must have kept my number from when we were in the modelling contest. U bully, getting your midget friend 2 do ur dirty work 4 u but hve removd page from facebook in case she makes truble 4 me. But I have not forgtten u or what u did to me. u r a bully. I hate u and ur stupid simpering face.

I felt sick as I read the words which had such hate in them. *Amazing*, I thought. *I haven't even done or said anything and yet she's the one accusing me of being a bully*. My first instinct was to delete the text and I was about to do so when I remembered what a visiting policeman had told us in school one day last term. He'd come into the school to do a talk about cyber-bullying and told us to keep emails and texts as evidence in case they were ever needed. Keira had been smart enough to remove the Facebook page before I had printed out a copy but I could save the text. I prayed that I wouldn't need to use it though and that she would leave me alone.

Don't think about it or her. I mustn't let her get to me, I told myself, though I knew that it was too late. She already had.

After supper, when the boys were tucked up in bed, I went down to the beach with my *Who Am I?* note-book. It was still light and I felt like some alone time, so I found a quiet spot, got out my notebook and sat down to look out over the sea.

Keira's text immediately began to play on loop in my mind. *You're a bully. I hate you and your stupid simpering face.* What she'd written hurt. I cursed inwardly that I'd let her get to me again. I so wished Pia was with me. I sent her a quick text to thank her for sending the message to Keira. She was such a good friend, always looking out for me. She seemed so far away in Denmark. At least she'd be returning to London tomorrow and I only had a few more days in Bournemouth, so soon we'd be able catch up properly. Pia wouldn't have let the text affect her, which is probably why Kiera targeted me and not her.

Why does she hate me so much? I asked myself. I searched my mind for anything that I could have done or said to her over the years, thinking right back to when we lived on the same street. Had I done something unforgiveable? Maybe I'd been insensitive. Maybe it was my fault she had a vendetta against me, but I couldn't think of anything. Was it just that sometimes people didn't get you and no matter how you behaved or what you said, they would interpret it differently? Maybe it was just that simple. I thought about what Mrs Callahan had said to us before we broke up from school. *Who are you?* I asked myself that question. *Who am I?* I knew I wasn't a bully, despite what Keira had said, so did that make me a victim? I jotted down some words under the heading, Who am I?

Hurt. Strong. Sensitive. Vulnerable.

Is it possible to be all those things at the same time? I wondered, then added some others.

Changing. Confused. Clear.
Schizophrenic.

'You're looking thoughtful,' said a voice behind me.

I turned to see Connor and Raffy. Raffy bounded over and greeted me as if I was his long lost best friend.

'Hi,' I said to both of them and gave Raffy's head a stroke.

'You looked miles away.'

'Just thinking about something. I wondered if we might bump into each other while we were staying down here.'

Connor nodded. 'I had a feeling we might. I have a philosophy about meeting people on my travels. If you're meant to meet them again, you always do.'

I smiled, liking the fact that the subtext of his statement was that I was one of the people he was meant to meet again. 'So how's your visit to Bournemouth been?' I asked.

'Good,' said Connor. 'What about you? What've you been up to?'

'I've been busy being Nanny McPhee,' I said. Connor looked puzzled. 'You know, in the films?'

Connor shook his head. 'Haven't seen them.'

'She's a nanny with a wart on her nose. I've been looking after my two young cousins. Holiday job sort of thing.'

'Ah,' said Connor and looked closely at my face. 'Wart on her nose? Do you have one?'

'Only metaphorically.'

He laughed. 'A metaphorical wart? Is that what you were thinking about?'

I nodded, then got the giggles. 'Sorry. I'm talking gobbledygook.'

Connor shook his head. 'Too right. Girls. I'll never understand them. So, do you want to take a walk? Maybe get a drink somewhere?' He pointed along the beach. 'There are some great cafés further along.'

'Sure,' I replied, got up and brushed sand off. I'd been working hard. I deserved a bit of time off. It would be nice to have some company my own age, especially company so drop dead gorgeous as Connor's.

As we walked along the sand, we chatted about our lives, what music we liked, who our friends were, and I found Connor really easy to talk to. He seemed genuinely interested in who I was and what I was into.

'And what do you want to do at uni?' he asked as he let Raffy off the lead. Once free, the dog raced off along the beach.

'That's the big question,' I said. 'No idea. Not child-minding, that much I do know. Far too exhausting and I don't think that I'm very good at it.'

I told him about the sink plunger episode and he cracked up laughing. 'Still, you have some time, don't you? You don't have to put in applications yet?'

'No. But we're expected to have some idea,' I replied. 'Maybe I'll do something creative. Maybe write. I don't know.'

'I didn't know for ages what I wanted to do,' said Connor. 'I did a foundation course in art. It was really good because we got to try out various different mediums before making our final choice. I found I loved photography. The classes weren't like work or school, if you know what I mean, more like my favourite hobby and I couldn't get enough of it. Is there anything you feel like that about?'

Shopping, snogging, fashion, I thought but didn't say so in case I sounded shallow. 'Er ... what I'm into keeps changing,' I replied. 'Maybe media.'

'Don't stress it,' said Connor. 'It'll come clear. Sometimes what comes first is what you *don't* want to do – like you said you don't want to do child-minding – and that helps you narrow it down.'

'Oh, I can give you a list of those. Banker, doctor, lawyer. I think I'd like to be rich, though.'

'Why?' Connor asked.

'More options. More freedom.' I thought about the life that JJ and Alisha had. There was no doubt it was super fab. Who wouldn't want what they had? 'Don't you want to be rich?'

'Not really. I mean, I don't want to be poor. I'd like to have a home, pay the bills and so on, but I'm not bothered about being wealthy. As long as I can play sport, walk Raffy, hang out with good mates, stuff like that. A walk on a beach on a cold day with Raffy, then a café for a hot cup of coffee and a bacon sarnie and to sit and watch the waves, that's my idea of heaven. I really wouldn't want much more. Fancy cars, watches, designer clothes, you can keep them. They don't float my boat.'

'Would you like to meet my father?' I said. 'I think he'd like you.'

Connor looked puzzled.

'And my Aunt Maddie, she'd like you too.'

Connor began to look worried.

I laughed. 'Just joshing,' I said. 'Hey, don't look so worried. I don't really want you to meet my family. Just Dad's always on about having the right values, realising where true happiness lies. And Aunt Maddie, well, she's Queen of Miss Do Right. My headmistress too, in fact, she's given us a project on it for over the holidays.'

'And you, Jess? Where do you think happiness lies?' Connor asked.

I thought for a moment. My happiest times? 'Easy. Being with mates. Being with the right people, and I count Dave, my cat, in that group. Doesn't really matter where.'

Connor nodded as if he agreed, then he got out a whistle. I noticed that I hadn't said being with JJ and felt a twinge of guilt, though spending time with him was high on the list. Connor blew his whistle and moments later, Raffy came bounding over to rejoin us.

'You've got him well trained,' I said.

Connor nodded. 'Works every time. I always carry it in case he goes off somewhere and I can't find him. I'd tried to use it on an ex-girlfriend once, she was always wandering off, like if we went shopping, I'd turn around and she'd be gone, but she soon told me where to go.'

I laughed. 'I think I'm with her there, like, have you never heard of mobile phones?'

'Point taken,' said Connor with a grin. He put Raffy back on his lead and we walked on until we came across a café bar with a deck overlooking the sea where we joined the many people hanging out enjoying the last of the sun.

I looked after Raffy and Connor went to get us drinks – a lager for him and Coke for me – and we stayed and continued our conversation with Connor telling me all about his love of photography. I heard my phone bleep a few times that someone had sent me a text but I didn't look. I could catch up on them later.

It was only when the sun began to disappear that I checked my watch. 'Oh my God, the time!' I gasped.

'Problem?' asked Connor.

'Not really, just I didn't let anyone know where I was going. I'd better get back.'

'I'll walk with you,' said Connor.

When we got outside the bar, I finally checked my messages. Five messages from Uncle John, each one growing more and more agitated. 'I'm for it when I get back,' I said.

'Er … possibly before that,' Connor said and nudged me to look over at the road. 'I've got a feeling that man might be looking for you.'

I glanced over to where he was looking to see an irate Uncle John getting out of his car.

I tried dodging down behind the wall to our left. 'I am so in the doghouse,' I said. 'Can he see me?'

Connor nodded. 'Seen and coming this way. You could always try burying yourself in the sand.'

I frantically started digging, much to the delight of Raffy who joined in with enthusiasm.

Happiness is:
Tucked up on a sofa with my little cousins fresh out of their bath and smelling of soap and watching kids' TV and eating crisps.
Hanging out with a cool boy, chatting and laughing.
Sitting on a beach in a warm breeze, looking out at the sea.

Unhappiness is:
One freaked-out relative going ballistic because I didn't call to say where I was.

Getting sand in my clothes when
trying to hide.
Dad telling me I am soooo grounded
when I get back to London.

8

Diary of a Slave Girl

Six-thirty a.m.: I thought there was a rule in the holidays for teenagers that there is only one six-thirty in a day, and that is in the evening. My dad has sadly not heard of this rule and woke me up at six-thirty in the *morning* with a cup of tea. On a Saturday too. Later in the day, Pia (whose mum had also woken her at the same time) called one of those child cruelty lines to complain about being made to slave over the weekend, but whoever answered the phone told her to stop wasting their time.

I was back in London and in at the deep end workwise. When Dad heard that I'd been out late with a boy, he and Uncle John had a big row, with Dad telling Uncle John that he obviously couldn't be trusted to look after a teenage girl. Uncle John was so mad he put me on the first train back to London. Dad could barely speak to me when I got back and just told me that I wouldn't be leaving the apartment block for 'quite some time'. Luckily Connor had given me his mobile number when we were chatting in the café, before Uncle John had appeared on the beach, so I was able to call him and give him an update. I'd felt conflicted when I'd given him my number and email address as to whether I should tell him about JJ or not. I decided against it in the end. It wasn't as if Connor had asked me out on a date or anything, so what was there to say? It might have come across as weird if I'd started filling him in on my relationship status when we'd only just met.

In prison in my own home, I texted him on the night I'd got back.

Will call you when I'm back in London, he'd texted back. Chin up.

Seven a.m.: Covered in plastic overalls and rubber gloves (not my best look unless trying to get off with an alien or person with a rubber fetish), Pia and I hosed, washed and waxed a fleet of cars whilst I told her the hiding in the sand story for the tenth time. She loved it.

'It's not fair though, P. I wasn't doing anything wrong,' I said. 'I was only out with a strange boy late at night in a strange town. What's wrong with that?'

Pia didn't answer. She just gave me one of her disapproving, disappointed looks. She'd make a good headmistress.

Eleven a.m.: Coffee and a biscuit followed by a group howl, or more precisely, a duet howl by Pia and me. She's been reading a self-help book and there's a chapter on a method called 'primal screaming'. The book says that it's best to let all anxiety and stress out in a big scream rather than keep it in. We decided to do wolf howling instead of primal screaming, in fact Pia's going to write her own book about it called *Release Your Inner Hound Without Going Barking Mad*. She has loads of methods for letting out stress. It felt great to yowl with no holding back. '*AwahwoOOO—*'

Sadly, Mr Sawtell appeared mid-howl (we were in his underground car park – great for echoes) and said something very rude to us about shutting up. Pia told

him all about the therapy but he looked totally unim-
pressed. He said his therapy was 'a pie and a pint on
a Friday night' and we were to get back to work and
stop frightening the neighbours.

Eleven-fifteen a.m.: Back to work till one. My delicate
lady's hands are getting ruined.

A text came through from Keira whilst Pia and I
were having a tea break. I c u r back, it said. I thought
there was a strange smell in London again.

'That's a bit freaky,' I said. 'It makes it sound as if
she knows I've been away.'

'She's just trying to get you to react,' said Pia.
'Ignore her. She's a sad loser.' Pia put her fists up and
boxed the air. 'Anyway, I'm here to protect you.'

I had to laugh at the idea of Pia as my bodyguard as
I switched my phone off and tried to put any images
of Keira stalking me out of my mind.

One p.m.: A quick sandwich and then we reported to
Pia's mum at the spa. We were given more overalls, a
bucket and a mop. Pia wrapped her hair up in a towel
turban and, when her mum disappeared, she began to
do a mop dance – our version of pole dancing but not
quite as sexy. Of course I joined in straight away. We

had quite a good routine worked out, I thought. Three steps to the right, three to the left, mop in left hand, dance around it, stomp, stomp and push the mop across the floor in a smooth skidding motion.

'We could try for the next *Britain's Got Talent* with this,' I said.

Pia nodded. 'I can see it catching on nationwide.'

Off we went again, to the left, to the right, stomp, stomp, glide right ... into Mrs Carlsen. *A good job she's not going to be on the panel of judges*, I thought when I saw her face. She didn't seem to appreciate our creative method of floor cleaning at all and told us to 'stop messing about and get on with it'. A couple of residents – an American man and his wife, from the fifth floor – came down to use the pool. They totally ignored us and treated us as if we were invisible, which I found especially amazing when Pia blew up one of her rubber gloves and put it on her head.

As I continued to work and dusted and cleaned the wall of mirrors at the back of the spa, I felt quite emotional watching the residents come out of the changing rooms in big towelling gowns, because the spa is where JJ and I used to hang out. He loves to swim and when he heard that I was a good swimmer, he requested that I be allowed to join him and pace him. Dad agreed – the policy of Porchester Park is what a resident wants, a resident gets – so the spa is where JJ and I got to know each other. It's also where he first asked me out so will always have romantic associations for me. Being there with him seemed like a long time ago now and he was so far away. I felt his absence like a dull ache in my stomach. I put the back of my hand up to my forehead à la tragic heroine. 'O, how painful my memories are of happier times here.' I said it in the kind of clipped English accent that you hear in old black and white movies and pronounced happier as 'heppier'.

'Get over it,' said Pia and she pointed to the mirror. 'And you've missed a spot.' Sometimes she can be just like her mother and very unsympathetic.

Three p.m.: We reported to the kitchen in the hotel next door for washing-up duty. More rubber gloves. Pia and I quickly got a good system going as I washed and she dried. We set ourselves targets and tried to see how many plates could we do in a minute. It got to be quite good fun.

After hundreds of plates, it didn't feel like such good fun.

Pia took two large plates and held them up, first behind her ears – 'Mickey Mouse,' she said – then positioned them in front of her eyes – 'Elton John,' – and lastly she held them in front of her chest – 'Katie Price.'

After washing up, we laid tables for dinner in the dining room, then at last we were done. Pia went off to collapse and watch telly. I went home to Skype JJ. I really wanted to see his face after having been in the spa earlier. I wanted to remind myself that he was real, I hadn't dreamt it and I wasn't invisible to people in his world.

Seven p.m.: Make-up on, hair tied back, ready to talk to JJ. When his camera came on, he looked amazing and so did the location. A light, airy apartment looking out over the ocean. A million miles away from busy, dusty Knightsbridge. However, despite the gorgeous location, he looked stressed.

'How's it going with your grandfather?' I asked.

'He's stable but not good. The doctors are making him as comfortable as possible.'

I wished there was something I could say to make him feel better, then I remembered how grateful I was when Mum was ill and Pia chatted away about

normal stuff because it took my mind off the awful-
ness of the situation. I told him all about my holiday
job, and after five minutes he was cracking up laughing, especially when I told him about the mop dance
and Pia with the inflated rubber glove on her head.

'God, I miss you guys,' he said and gave me a look
that tugged on my heart.

'Me too,' I said. And it wasn't just JJ I missed. Much
though I hated to admit it, I missed the access he gave
me to the wonderful world he lived in. I'd realised
since he left how unusual the Lewis family was in
befriending Charlie, Pia and I. Other rich residents
and their teenagers passed us in the hall or corridor as
if we didn't even exist and I could see for certain that
none of them would be inviting me up to their apartments for a freshly squeezed grape juice or evening in
one of their private cinemas like Alisha and JJ had
done. I was staff and to be ignored.

'How's Alisha?' I asked.

'Better since Prasad visited,' he said.

'Prasad has been over?!'

JJ nodded. 'A short trip. He's gone on to New York
with his mom.'

I was glad Alisha had managed to see Prasad after
all, but the fact that he'd just flown over to see her

was another reminder that my world was so different from theirs. The possibility of me hopping over to see JJ was not going to happen, not on my pocket money, even boosted with my recent earnings. Skype would have to do for JJ and me, but at least it meant I got to see him.

When we finished our call, I turned my mobile back on to see if Pia had been in touch, and a text came through almost immediately. But it wasn't from Pia, it was another message from Keira.

Just 2 let u know that I haven't 4gotten u. I will b watching u. u silly cow.

I so felt like writing something back but remembered Pia's advice from the morning, and also earlier in the year, when Kiera had sent abusive messages. 'Ignore her. And do NOT engage because then she'll know she's hooked you and got a reaction.'

I knew she was right, so quickly pressed *save* then turned my phone off. I really wasn't in the mood for Kiera and her games. I sat and looked out of the window for a few moments. The text had totally ruined the good feeling I'd got from seeing JJ. I got up to look for my rucksack. It was under my desk where I'd thrown it when I'd got home on the last day of term. I remembered that the man who'd come in to school to do the talk about bullying had left us with a leaflet. I hadn't looked at it at the time, but I pulled it out now. There was a website on the leaflet: www.beatbullying.org.

I sat back at my computer and went to the site. Right on the home page was the story of a girl who'd been bullied online. I identified immediately with her and as I read her and other people's accounts and how they'd handled it, I felt like I wasn't alone. The site gave some really good advice and there was also a link to another site called www.cybermentors.org.

CyberMentors – cool name for a band, I thought as I clicked through. *They even sound like some kind of superhero.* An image of Pia dressed in superman clothes, arriving at the scene of trouble, flashed through my mind, like, 'Yo, CyberMentor is here,' she would say as she knocked bullies' heads together – *kapow, kapow, schlosh, bash.*

Pia would make a good CyberMentor and I knew I was lucky to have her as my own personal one.

I had a quick look around the site. It seemed there was some kind of online program to talk to someone in confidence or send a message if I wanted to. The best thing was that a lot of the CyberMentors were young people who had experienced bullying themselves, so would know exactly what I was going through. *What a brilliant site*, I thought. Just knowing they were there and that I wasn't the only one to have to deal with something like this made me feel better. I thought about registering and having a chat to someone there, but Dave came in and settled at the end of my bed. 'Good idea,' I said and got up to find my PJs. Five minutes later, I was fast asleep.

Most of my days in slavery were the same, and at the end of the first week I went into Dad's office, saluted and stood to attention. 'Permission for day off, sir,' I asked in a fake military voice.

He raised an eyebrow as if to say most unfunny. 'Of course you can have a day off, Jess. You can stay home ... and clean.'

I raised my eyebrow back at him in exactly the same manner he had just done to me. 'Most amusing, Dad.'

'Just kidding,' he said. 'Sure, take the day off tomorrow, you've earned it. I'll get some agency people to come in and cover you and Pia.'

The next day, I slept until eleven-thirty – which was bliss! Then Pia came over and we sat at the breakfast bar chatting and drinking milky coffees. Double bliss. It felt like we were on the best holiday ever.

'One thing about working is that it really makes you appreciate time off,' I said.

'Happiness,' said Pia, 'is to do with contrast. To have a day off when you've been going at it. To have a rest when you're tired and on the opposite end, to have something to do when you're bored.'

'A drink when you're thirsty, to be cool when you're too hot.'

'Why didn't we get it before? This is a big realisation to add to our happiness project. Happiness is all about contrast. Mrs Callahan will be well impressed!'

After our coffees, seeing as it was a lovely summer's day, we went out to lie in the back garden, taking magazines, water and suntan lotion with us. We put towels on the small bit of lawn out there and lay down to get well stuck in to some chill-out time.

'Your horoscope, madam,' said Pia as she lay back and opened her *Girl in the City* magazine. 'Uranus is at a strong angle to Jupiter, bringing unexpected news that will expand your horizons. Be open to the changes it brings.'

Just as I'd got comfy and Pia was about to read her stars, Dad appeared at the back door.

'Jess?'

I sat up. 'Yes.'

'Come inside a moment,' he said. 'I need a word with you.'

I groaned, wondering what I'd done. 'Oh God, here we go.'

'The unexpected,' said Pia. 'Let it begin.'

<u>Jess and Pia's latest rules of happiness:</u>

Time with mates is v. important.

Contrast brings happiness:

To get warmed up when you're freezing.

To cool down when you're hot.

Time off when you've been busy.

To have a project when you've been bored.

Time alone when you've had days with loads of people.

Time with loads of people when you've been alone.

Contrast, yeah? Get it?

9

Star-studded Opportunity

I left Pia in the garden and went in to talk to Dad.

'I'm aware that car washing and dish washing aren't really your thing,' Dad said when I got inside.

I nodded in agreement. 'Not my life's choice.'

'So you'll be pleased to know that I have something else to offer you.'

I tried to read his face. 'I'm not very good at ironing either.'

'Nothing like that. No. Stephanie Harper,' he said. 'She came to find me this morning. There's been a last minute problem with the arrangements for her book tour this week. The girl who was supposed to be accompanying her has broken her ankle so Stephanie's looking for someone to take her place.'

'Take her place?'

'Personal assistant for the week sort of thing, I think. She wants to see you about it. She'll fill you in.'

'She wants me to find her a PA? I ... I wouldn't know where to start.'

'No,' said Dad. 'She wants you to *be* her PA.'

I felt a rush of anxiety. 'PA? *Me*? But, Dad, I have no experience of anything like that.'

'I think you could do it. It's only for a week. Could be great work experience for you, Jess. She wants you to go up to see her in the Lewises' apartment and have a chat about it as soon as you can.'

'I'll get changed and go now,' I said and quickly went back outside to let Pia know what was happening.

'She must think I'm older than I look or something,' I said. 'I won't be able to do it.'

'No. It's so cool,' she said. 'Find out what she wants before you decide you can't do it. She might want you to make her sandwiches, get her coffee, something simple.'

'God, I feel so nervous.'

'Imagine you're Lady Gaga or someone mega confident while she's interviewing you.'

'Yeah right, maybe I should wear a dress made of ham like Lady G did once,' I called back to her. 'Will you come and help me get ready?'

'Course,' said Pia and she got up to come to my room and chat to me.

I got changed into my jeans and a shirt and looked in the mirror.

'Will this do?' I asked.

Pia glanced me over. 'Perfect, but ask Stephanie how she'd like you to dress for the job so it shows that you're willing to dress smarter if she feels it's required.'

I took a deep breath then went downstairs where Dad was waiting for me. I followed him into the reception where he telephoned up to Ms Harper that I was going to go up in the lift. I still felt so nervous. There was no way that someone like her would give me a job once she realised that my only work experience was car washing, babysitting and floor mopping.

Ms Harper opened the door to the Lewises' apartment and invited me to follow her into the living room. She was dressed in an ankle-length kaftan and another of her fabulous necklaces, this time a huge jade stone set in silver.

The place smells different, I thought as I went in.

When the Lewis family were there, the apartment smelt of an ocean breeze; now the scent was heavier and muskier, like fig or sandalwood. It felt weird to be there without JJ or Alisha, and I felt a wave of sadness at missing them, but told myself to smile and look positive. Stephanie indicated that I should sit on one of the cream sofas. I did as I was told and noticed that the usual glossy magazines on the coffee table had been removed and replaced by astrology magazines and various books about the stars and planets.

'Can I get you something to drink?' asked Ms Harper. 'A glass of apple juice, a herbal tea or do you want a cup of your English tea?'

'Juice will be fine, thanks.' I crossed my legs then uncrossed them, then folded my arms then unfolded them. I remembered Pia's advice to act like someone I knew would be confident. I quickly scanned my mind for confident people. The Prime Minister. President of America. Rhianna. The Queen. For some reason, the Queen stuck and immediately I sat up straighter. Ms Harper came back in with two glasses of juice, put them on the table in front of us and sat down. I did a Queen-like wave and nod.

'Are you OK, Jess?' Ms Harper asked.

'Quait well thank you, Ms Harper,' I said in my Queen type voice.

Ms Harper gave me a funny look and I felt myself blush. *What the heckity thump am I doing?* I asked myself. *Relax, you idiot.*

'First of all, I'd like you to call me Stephanie,' she said. 'And this isn't going to be a formal interview, so you can relax. So, Jess, any idea why I chose you?'

I shook my head.

'You know what my line of work is?' she asked.

'Astrology.'

Stephanie nodded. 'It is. I work with the stars, with symbols and signs and I believe it could have been a sign that you brought my case back to me that day in Harrods. That showed me I could trust you, Jess. And then we bumped into each other here. It's quite a coincidence that you live right here, in the same location as the one I'm staying in, don't you think?'

I nodded. 'When you put it like that, I guess so.' *Not exactly the same location though*, I thought as I gazed out of the floor-to-ceiling windows that looked out over Hyde Park from the designer living room that was almost the size of a tennis court.

'I take note of things like that in my life,' she continued. 'Plus the fact that you're a Sagittarian and I'm

Aquarian means we should get along nicely. Now, tell me, what time were you born, do you know?'

I nodded. 'Four in the morning. I remember because my mum used to tease me about keeping her awake all night.'

'And where were you born?'

'Here in London.'

She asked what year and then opened the laptop that was on the table in front of her and typed some details into her computer. I wasn't sure what she was doing but decided not to be too inquisitive. She was the one interviewing me, so she should ask the questions. After a few minutes, she looked up and beamed.

'Excellent,' she said. 'I was just looking at your birthchart. Sagittarius with Gemini rising and the moon in Taurus. And you have your Mars in Capricorn – that means you are a hard worker. Yes, I think we will get along very well.'

I nodded as if I understood but she could have been talking Greek to me.

'As your father may have told you,' she continued, 'I need an assistant to help me for a week or so. I'm over here to promote my book *Signs of our Times* and I will be doing several interviews and visiting a number of bookshops. I need someone to come with me to help with the signings, organise the queues, and make sure we have some decent food to eat. Usually all I tend to get offered is sandwiches, biscuits and cake and I'd be the size of a house by the time I went home if I didn't eat something healthy once in a while. I want a companion really, but one who can do a few jobs as well. Do you think you could do that?'

'Is the tour already organised? I mean, I wouldn't have to do that, would I?'

'The schedule is already in place. You may have to do some phoning ahead to confirm a few details, but really it's just about being with me on the day. So a yes or no?'

I felt a rush of adrenalin as a mental picture of me accompanying her around the country flashed through my mind. 'Yes. I think I could. I'd love to.' I meant it too. 'Don't you want to know what my qualifications are?'

Stephanie shook her head. 'I've seen your chart and that lets me see your basic traits – all good. As I said, I already know I can trust you and Mrs Lewis gave you a great recommendation. What do you say we give it a go for a few days, see how we get on, then take it from there?'

'Great. Er … when did you want me to start?'

'Monday too soon for you? I'm doing a signing at a bookshop in town. I know it's all very last minute but the girl who was supposed to come with me fell and broke her ankle.'

I thought of my alternative: the sinks full of dishes, floors to be mopped and cars to be washed. 'Oh no,' I said. 'Not too soon at all. And do you want me to dress a particular way?'

'Smart but casual,' said Stephanie. 'It's the book world so you'll be fine in the sort of thing you're wearing right now. Any other questions?'

I shook my head. My imagination was in full flood picturing me accompanying Stephanie around. Her PA. It was going to be so glamorous.

Stephanie smiled. 'Don't you want to know how much I'm going to pay?' she asked.

'Oh that. Oh yes, I suppose so.'

Stephanie wrote a figure on a piece of paper and pushed it towards me. 'Would that be acceptable?'

I took a deep breath. 'For a week?'

Stephanie laughed. 'For each day,' she said.

I almost fell off the sofa.

10

A Message from JJ

I took the lift down and almost skipped my way back to my garden where Pia was still basking in the sun.

'Do you mind?' I asked, after I'd told her my good news.

'Course not, idiot. I'm really pleased for you, and anyway, Henry will be back next week so I can do car washing with him,' she said. 'What I mean is, it will be fine working with him.'

Unlike Charlie, Henry was returning to England from the boys' holiday earlier so that he could earn some money to help see him through uni in September. Even so, I knew Pia was trying to make the best of me abandoning her. 'I'll get you something really fab with my wages,' I said. 'That is, if I last beyond the first day.'

'No need. We're mates so your good news is my good news,' said Pia, then she grinned. 'I'll email a wish list over, though.'

Just at that moment, my phone bleeped that I had a text.

R u free 2 go 2 skype? JJ, it said.

I texted back. B there in a sec.

I explained to Pia that JJ was going to call and left her sunning herself and headed straight to my computer. Moments later, JJ was on my screen. He looked pretty low so I presumed that the news about his grandfather was still not good.

'Hey,' I said. 'You OK?'

He nodded but I wasn't convinced. 'Guess where I've just been,' I said.

He shrugged. 'Harrods?'

'Up to your apartment. Stephanie Harper wanted to see me.'

JJ smiled. 'Oh yeah. She was talking to Mom about you.'

'It was weird being up there without you. She's offered me a job!'

JJ nodded. 'I thought she might. Mom gave you a glowing reference. You going to take it?'

'It's going to be a trial first to see if we get on, so maybe no more mop dancing for me.'

'That's a shame, but I want to see that dance when we next meet.'

'Did you put your mum up to getting me the job?'

'Not really. But I told her some of what you'd been going through with, er ... the mop dance and all, then she just happened to be talking to Stephanie later and she told Mom that she wanted an assistant. The big thing, Jess, is that she wants someone she can trust. She doesn't want to go through a whole load of try-outs with people at this short notice. Mom suggested you and she was over the moon.'

'Ha ha,' I said. 'Over the moon. That's good for an astrologer.'

'Oh yeah, right,' said JJ. 'But apparently you had already met in Harrods or something?'

'Yes. She'd left her case behind and I caught up with her and gave it back to her.'

JJ nodded. 'Stephanie would like that. She's one of those people who doesn't believe anything happens by coincidence. You know the type. To her, everything is fated. It's probably all in written her stars for July.' He was silent for a while.

'Are you really OK, JJ?' I asked.

'Sure. Yes. No.' JJ shrugged a shoulder. 'Jess, I have something to say. I ... I'm trying to find the right words.'

I felt my heart sink. 'Is it about your grandpa?'

'Sort of. It's to do with him. He's doing slightly better, stable at least, but ... This is the thing. Mom and Pop want to stay here indefinitely to be close, in case ... you know.'

I nodded. I understood. 'Until he's better? That makes sense.'

'The doctors don't see him improving in the near future; it's going to be a long road and Mom and Pop want to be there on it with him. As you know, the plan was for us to come back to the UK, I was all set go to university over there in the fall and Alisha to go back to home-studying but ...'

I felt my heart sink even more. I knew what he was going to say before he said it. 'You're all going to stay over there?'

JJ nodded. 'I am so sorry, Jess. Sorry for what this means for you and me. We all sat down and talked yesterday and Mom said if I start my course here, she wants me to finish here, no chopping and changing. She's always been against us travelling too much, and if we stay it also means that Alisha can go back to her old school.'

'I bet she's pleased about that.' I knew Alisha had missed her American friends when she was in England and had felt isolated being home-schooled. She'd be so happy to be back with her old mates.

'She is. But then Prasad is in the UK, so it has its downside too because she won't see so much of him. She wants to talk to you later but I wanted to speak to you first.'

'But we can still see each other, can't we? Holidays? Won't you ever be over this way? What's going to happen to your apartment?'

JJ looked sad. 'Not sure. We may rent it out, we may sell. Stephanie's only there for part of the summer and it seems a shame for it to be empty after that. Mom said she's not making any decisions about it for at least a year. And yes, we could see each other but Jess ...'

'Yes?'

'I thought long and hard about this last night. You're fifteen. I'm eighteen. You know what you mean to me ... the connection we have is really special, but it's not fair of me to ask you not to see anyone else while I'm over here because, realistically, we might only see each other a few times a year, if that.'

I gasped. JJ was telling me that I meant a lot to him. That was good, wasn't it? He was telling me that what we had was really special. Also good. But he was also telling me that we were over. My first proper boyfriend and we'd lasted barely three months. I couldn't get my head round it.

'Are you OK, Jess?'

I nodded. I wished that we weren't on Skype because he could see my face and I was never very good at hiding my feelings. 'Yes. No. I ... I don't know what to say. I ...'

JJ's face on the screen reflected my own. He looked so upset. I couldn't take in what he had just said, and the implications. The idea of not hanging out with him, or having his arms around me again or being able to kiss him, it hurt. It hurt *big time*. 'I hate Skype. You're right there in front of me but you're not.'

He nodded. 'All I want to do is hold you right now but it's just as you said, we can't do cyber hugs or kisses. We know we'll always be special to each other,

Jess. No one can take away what we had when we were together.'

I nodded. I wanted to cry but didn't want him to see me. It would be hard enough for him with his grandfather being so ill and his family all so concerned without me blubbing over him and making him even more miserable. He needed my support not my freaking out. 'We can still talk, can't we? And be friends?'

'More than friends,' he said. 'I know it hurts right now, but you see the sense of it, don't you?'

'I guess. Not really. Oh, I don't know, JJ. Until now, I've been hanging on to the fact that you'd be coming back. It's a lot to take in, you staying in the States, as well as ... us being over. I ... I've got to go now, Dad's calling me,' I lied. 'Stay in touch, yeah? And tell Alisha I'll speak to her later.'

'I will,' he said. 'Love you.'

It was the first time he'd used the L word. 'You too,' I said – then pressed *end call* and burst into tears.

11

An End and a Start

'So it's *over* over?' asked Pia after I'd filled her in on
my conversation with JJ.

I nodded. 'But I spoke to Alisha soon after JJ and
she's in the same situation with Prasad. In fact, it's
even more difficult with him because he lives in India
and goes to school in the UK. However, they're not
going to let the distance get in their way and are
going to try and make it work. His parents are often
in the States on business, so if he's not at school he
can go with them and see Alisha.'

Pia shook her head. 'So it's not the same situation.
Prasad has access to a private jet. You have access to

the number 126 bus, which will take you as far as the Hammersmith flyover.'

'JJ has access to a private jet,' I argued.

'No, he doesn't. His mum and dad do. And you just said yourself that Prasad's parents have to travel to the USA on business. Either way, Prasad, Alisha or JJ, they're in different worlds to us. We've always known that. In the meantime, your life isn't over. You have the offer of a fabtastic job and it's not like JJ dumped you because he didn't like you anymore. He's done the noble thing. He's saying goodbye because he doesn't want to hold you back. I think that's incredibly considerate.'

'Doesn't feel like it,' I said.

'Let it go,' said Pia. 'At least for now. Nothing is ever set in stone and I'm sure you'll meet JJ again some time. Besides, you have other things to think about, like what are you going to wear tomorrow for your first day as a high-flying PA?'

We spent the rest of the evening going through my wardrobe for the right outfit for my new job. That, and eating a whole tub of ice cream between us. 'When the going gets tough, the tough eat ice cream' is one of Pia's many mottos, and when she saw how distraught I still was after her 'your life is still fabtastic' talk, she went out and bought double chip vanilla with extra fudge.

'Maybe it's a case of right boy, wrong time,' she said as she spooned big creamy mounds into a bowl. 'Just because it's over for now, doesn't mean it's over forever. One thing we've both seen from living here at Porchester Park is that distance needn't be an obstacle for people who have access to private jets. OK, his parents are going to be sensible in term time, but there are still the holidays, Jess. And there are still other cute boys around. JJ knows that too, he doesn't want to hold you back, but I think it shows that he's sure of what the two of you have – he can let you go temporarily. It's really mature of him if you think about it.'

By the time she'd finished, I was feeling more hopeful that this didn't mean it was over forever between me and JJ, and my future didn't seem so gloomy. Pia's so good at always seeing the bright side, and after her talk I was well cheered up and we got into picking my clothes for the morning. In the end, we settled on my jeans, denim Converse and a pale blue top with daisies on it that I got from Topshop.

'And if you wear your hair back, it will make you look more sophisticated,' she said. 'Especially with a strong lip colour.'

I laughed. 'Agony aunt and make-up artist, is there no end to your talents?'

Pia shook her head. 'Nope and I want you to remember that for when you're famous because I could be your PA then.'

'Deal,' I said.

Once the clothes were laid out for the next day and Pia had gone home, I went to check my emails. There was one from someone called Bethany outlining the book tour schedule for the week and saying she would call me to go over it and see if I had any questions. I couldn't help but feel a rush of excitement as I glanced at the itinerary. I printed out the pages and made a note of the times and where we had to be and when.

There was also an email from Connor saying he was back in London and asking if I would like to meet up. I felt torn. *JJ and I are no longer an item*, I thought, *so I wouldn't be cheating. On the other hand, our break-up has only just happened and my feelings for JJ haven't changed. It feels too soon to get into another relationship.*

I called Pia, the fount of all wisdom in my life.

'There's no harm in meeting up – he might just want to be mates, and it might do you some good to get out there and have some fun. Remember the rule to be cool and not too available in the beginning.'

After talking to Pia, I emailed Connor back: I'd like to meet up but am about to start a new job accompanying a famous astrologer on a book tour.

He replied: So you'll be starry-eyed. Haha. Where is ur first stop? Might c u there. Raffy is missing you.

Well, he's certainly not playing by the rule to be cool in the beginning, I thought as I let him know where I'd be the next morning. I switched off my computer and got ready for bed.

Just as I was settling down and Dave had taken up his usual position at the end of my bed, Dad called up that there was a call for me. I thought it was JJ or Alisha, but when I went to the phone, I found it turned out to be Bethany, the woman from Stephanie's publisher who had sent the schedule through.

'I feel just awful about letting Stephanie down,' she said, 'and all our other PR people are out on the road with authors. Stephanie wouldn't hear about us looking for someone else, insisting that she had found her girl.'

'Yes, well, I really hope that I'm going to do a good job for her,' I said.

'All your travel arrangements are booked. I've organised for the tickets you need to be sent to the reception at Porchester Park tomorrow morning and any journeys by car are sorted out too. It's all there on the schedule. So, any questions?'

'Well, er ... Stephanie didn't exactly say what she wanted me to do apart from accompany her and organise the queues ...'

'You have done this before, haven't you?'

'Um ... no, I haven't.'

'So what job experience do you have in the book world?'

'Er ... none really, I'm still at school.'

'At *school*! How old are you exactly?'

'Fifteen. I'll be sixteen in December.' There was a long pause at the other end of the phone. 'Are you still there, Bethany?'

I heard a long exhalation of breath. 'Let me call you back.'

I put the phone down. *Well, that's the end of that*, I thought. I just knew she was going to call Stephanie and tell her I was too young. My first job and I was going to get sacked before I'd even started. That had to be a record.

Sure enough, the phone rang about fifteen minutes

later. Bethany again. 'Stephanie said to meet her at the front of the building at nine tomorrow morning.' Her voice sounded clipped.

'So I'm not sacked?'

'No. Stephanie wouldn't hear of it. She said it's meant to be.'

'Meant to be?'

'Your horoscope told her more than any CV, she said. It's destined. Fate. Stephanie's big on all that.' From Bethany's tone of voice, it didn't sound as though she felt the same way.

'I *will* do my best.'

'You better had,' she said, 'because it's my reputation that's on the line here. I want you to report to me at the end of every day, and if you have any questions, any problems, you call me. You got that?'

'Got it,' I said. I was glad we weren't on Skype because she'd have seen me stick my tongue out at her. She sounded really bossy.

Life is constantly changing, I thought when I finally settled down for bed. *My relationship with JJ is over. A new one may be about to begin with Connor. A horrible job, then the offer of an amazing one. Keira turning up out of the blue and causing problems. Who knows what tomorrow will bring?*

'Meow,' said Dave from the end of my bed.
Sometimes, I swear that cat reads my mind.

Happiness is:
An unexpected opportunity coming out of the blue.
Sharing a tub of ice cream with a best mate.
Lying in the sun on a well-deserved morning off.
A boy I like saying he loves me.

Unhappiness is:
Not being able to be with the boy who loves me.

12

The Tour Begins

Monday morning and I was up and dressed early. I made myself a cup of tea, and a piece of toast and raspberry jam which I hardly tasted, then I went to the front of the reception area to collect the tickets and wait for Stephanie and the car. As always, the area smelt divine from the Jo Malone candles they burn there all day and I noticed the flowers of the day on the glass cabinet in the centre were an enormous display of white orchids.

Yoram was on the door for the morning shift. He's ex-army and is lean and fit-looking. As always, he looked immaculate with short hair, a smart black suit and highly polished black shoes. He was never friendly, unlike Didier, the other security guy. I always felt that Yoram disapproved of my friendship with the Lewises, as if he felt it was inappropriate for me to mix with the residents. He gave me the briefest of nods and didn't ask what I was doing there. I knew that Dad would have told him about me working for Stephanie already; Yoram made it his business to know everything that was going on at the apartment block.

As I waited, the French family from the third floor came down for their car and the teenage boy who had ignored me last week when I was dressed in my cleaner's overalls, checked me out as he went past and gave me a flirty look. It felt good to be on the other side of things again, instead of the invisible girl in the rubber gloves with a mop.

At nine-fifteen, a sleek black Mercedes drew up outside. JJ had told me that they were loaning it to Stephanie as well as their apartment. I peeked into the front. A young man with blond hair under his chauffeur's cap was behind the wheel. I didn't recognise him from when I'd travelled with the Lewises and realised, they must have taken their drivers with them to the USA.

Five minutes later, Stephanie came down and Yoram opened the back door of the car for her. She was dressed in a pale green linen dress and her usual silver jewellery, but despite her cool outfit, she looked in a flap and was weighed down with bags of books and papers.

'Best if you meet me upstairs next time, Jess,' she said as she handed me one bag, then got into the car. 'Just to check I've got everything. There's always so much to carry and remember at the last minute.'

'I'm so sorry. I should have thought of that,' I said as I got in after her. I noticed Yoram's expression. A slight raising of the eyebrow as if he was agreeing with her. I could just imagine his reaction when Dad had told him about me getting the job with Stephanie. He would have thought that I wasn't up to it. *I'll show you, Yoram*, I thought.

'Don't worry. You weren't to know, I should have asked you,' said Stephanie as the car pulled away. 'You'll get the hang of it.'

As we made our way to Piccadilly, Stephanie explained that one of the main things she wanted me to do was to manage the signing queue. *That should be easy peasy*, I thought. I'd been a prefect at school one term and had got good at getting people to stand in lines at school assembly. The other job she wanted me to do was to write the names people waiting in the queue on a Post-it note.

'And then will it be my job to stick the Post-it note in a book?' I asked as Stephanie handed me a small pad that she'd brought with her.

'Oh no,' said Stephanie. 'Your job is to quickly put the note on the cover of the book to be signed, then pass it to me so I can see how to spell each person's name. In busy shops, it's hard to hear the individual spellings sometimes.' She got out a piece of paper and wrote something before handing it to me. She had written, *Nicky, Nikki, Nicki, Nici, Niki, Nikky.* 'See? You can spell a really simple name so many different ways. You'll be saving me a lot of time if you write it down so I don't have to ask, then strain to hear.'

I nodded. 'Keep queue in order, write down names. Got it.'

'And watch my things. When I'm busy, I can't keep an eye on my bag or jacket. I have had things stolen before now.'

'OK.'

'Then, later, at the end of the day, you must send an update to Bethany,' said Stephanie. 'And always put a positive spin on it. A good PR person will make even a disaster sound like the best time ever.'

'Will do,' I said, though judging by the crowd already waiting in the rain outside the shop when we drew up, there was little chance of any of the signings being a disaster. The window display at the front right had been completely dedicated to Stephanie, with a huge life-size poster of her, and as soon as we got out of the car, someone in the waiting group recognised her and people started staring and nudging each other, looking at me as well as Stephanie. Despite my first-day job nerves, it felt exciting to be the centre of attention. We went inside and a young man with gelled-up red hair immediately came over to us, introduced himself as Barry, then took us to an area in the centre of the shop near the main stairs.

'I thought this would be a good place for you to sign,' he said. 'That way, we get the customers going up and down the stairs as well.' He pointed to a counter to our left which was piled high with Stephanie's books. 'People can buy there, then come over to the table here to get the books signed.'

We looked at the table and chair that had been set out and Stephanie beamed at him. 'Good thinking.

Now, Jess, you stand somewhere in between the counter and the table, OK? Post-it notes ready?'

I nodded and took up my place.

'Now, can I get you tea, coffee, water?' asked Barry.

'Peppermint tea, please,' said Stephanie as she took her place behind the desk.

Barry's face flushed. 'Oh, we don't have that,' he said.

'Never mind. Jess will get me some, won't you, Jess?' said Stephanie.

'Yes. Course.'

Barry dashed to the till and came back with a twenty-pound note which he handed to me.

'Make sure it's organic and hurry back,' said Stephanie.

'Right,' I said and raced to the front of the store. Once out on the pavement, I realised I hadn't a clue where I was going. I glanced up and down the busy, noisy road. I could see carpet shops and cafés stretched out in front of me. Where to go? Then I remembered. Fortnum and Mason! Of course. It was close by and was the poshest shop in London. It always had a great supply of rare teas and coffees and wasn't far away.

At that moment, the skies opened and there was a

torrential downpour. Within seconds, people were soaked and diving for shelter in shop doorways. I didn't want to keep Stephanie waiting so I ran as fast as I could to Fortnum's and into the ground floor. My hair was plastered to my head and dripping down my neck, but there was nothing I could do. I asked a doorman where the tea was and he pointed to the left of the shop whilst giving me a strange look, probably because I looked like I'd just got out of a swimming pool.

A few minutes later, I'd found the teas. I searched for peppermint teabags but couldn't find any. I spotted a counter with loose tea. Phew. They had organic peppermint. *This job is going to be OK after all. Shopping for tea, easy peasy*, I thought as I joined the queue. I tried to flick some of the rain out of my hair and unfortunately it hit an old Japanese lady behind me. She bashed me with her umbrella.

'Sorry,' I said.

'You very wet,' she said and pushed her way in front of me. She didn't look like someone to mess with so I let her go. I glanced at my watch and realised that I'd been gone ten minutes. The assistant at the counter seemed to be taking forever, chatting to her customers as she weighed tea leaves, and everyone was getting impatient. The queue nudged forward slowly and finally it was the turn of the Japanese lady. Halfway through being served, she changed her mind about what she wanted so the assistant had to start again. Finally she finished her order, but when she handed over her card for payment, her card wouldn't go through so the assistant had to call for verification.

I felt my palms starting to sweat. *Calm down*, I told myself. *I can't go back without the tea so there's no point in getting worked up.* I took a deep breath and inhaled the lovely smell of coffee that filled the air. *Coffee mixed with eau de damp clothes today*, I thought.

At last, the Japanese lady finished her business and the queue moved forward. *My turn*, I thought with relief but the assistant got caught up in finding something for her manager who butted in just as I was about to speak. I looked at my watch again. I'd been gone almost twenty minutes. Finally, it really was my turn. The assistant put my tea in a bag, took payment, then I legged it back to the bookshop as fast as I could.

The store had opened and was buzzing with activity, particularly over at the signing table. I couldn't see Stephanie anywhere, just a hoard of people, four or five circles deep. I muscled my way in to see that Stephanie was seated at the table in the middle of them, desperately trying to keep up with signing the books that were being thrust at her from left, right, behind and in front.

'Where have you been?' she demanded. 'I thought you'd run off.'

'Queue,' I said as I tried to catch my breath. 'Sorry. Where's Barry?'

'How would I know? Not organising the queue, that's for sure. You're going to have to do that.'

I looked at the mob around her. 'Er ... would you mind moving back, please?' I ventured to the people nearest me.

No one took any notice. So much for the brilliant plan for people to buy a book from Barry, give me their name for the Post-it note and then for Stephanie to sign the book before they moved on and away. It was pandemonium and Stephanie was looking at me pleadingly.

'Do something,' she said, as she scribbled her name in the next book that was thrust under her nose.

I moved round to what seemed to be the front of the crowd where there were two teenage boys. 'Who is the book to be signed for?' I asked.

'My mum,' said one of the boys. 'Anna Williams.'

'How do you spell that?' I asked and jotted down the name as he told me, placing the Post-it on the front of the book. As he moved forward, he turned to his mate. 'Signed copies could be worth something,' he said.

'More if she was dead,' said his friend and they both sniggered.

And she probably will be soon if this carries on, I thought as I watched more people join the crowd surging forward. People were still piling in the shop, Barry was nowhere to be seen and this was getting way out of control. I had to do something. I fought my way to the back of the crowd near the stairs and went up a couple so that I could see over everyone's head.

'Er ... excuse me,' I called. No-one even turned around. I tapped on one lady's shoulder. 'Excuse me, could you get in line?'

She looked at the huddle around Stephanie. 'What line?'

'You could make one,' I suggested.

The lady scoffed at me. 'Haven't time to wait,' she said and pushed ahead. I went back down the stairs and back to Stephanie's side. 'Are you OK?'

'Not really. I might have to leave if you don't do something,' she said as one of the teenage boys I'd seen earlier handed her a felt pen and asked if she would sign his forehead.

I tried talking to the crowd again. 'A single queue, please,' I said in a loud voice.

An elderly bald man gave me a look as if to say how pathetic I was.

'*Please* keep in a single line,' I said in a slightly louder voice. 'GET in line.'

'I've been queuing for ages,' said the old man who'd given me the look. '*You* get in line. Who do you think you are?'

'I'm Stephanie's PA,' I said.

The man looked me up and down and scoffed. 'Yeah and I'm the Pope,' he said. 'Now get in line like the rest of us.'

Behind him, I could see the Japanese lady from Fortnum's had joined the queue. She gave me another bash with her umbrella. It hurt.

'Ow,' I protested.

'You naughty queue jumper,' she said and she jostled me out of her way with her elbows. That hurt too. I could just see my report to Bethany later. *Stephanie Harper suffocated by flash mob in Piccadilly, London. Bookshop closed for health and safety reasons. Schoolgirl Jessica Hall held responsible for the chaos plus was arrested for biffing an old lady over the head.*

Suddenly, there was the sound of a loud whistle and

there was a moment of silence as everyone turned to see what it was.

'ORDER!' said a loud male voice. 'Either everyone gets in a *single* line or Ms Harper will be leaving. Can you not see that you're crowding her?'

I stood on tiptoe to see Connor with Raffy's whistle in his hand and Raffy by his side. He went and positioned himself on the stairs where I'd been earlier. 'The queue will resume to my right with the man in the blue jacket. Everyone else should line up behind him. Come on now, or you will all be asked to leave,' he said in a very firm voice. Amazingly, people responded to him and began to get in line. Connor walked over to the table where Stephanie was so I scooted over to join them.

'Are you all right, ma'am?' he asked. Stephanie nodded. 'I suggest we take a short break and come back when we have some crowd control,' Connor added.

'I'll be fine,' said Stephanie. 'And you are?'

'Friend of Jess's,' he said. 'Can I do anything?'

'Well, if you can keep the line in order that would be great and maybe get me some water,' said Stephanie.

'Coming up,' said Connor and he turned to me. 'Can you get that?'

I was so stunned to see him that I just nodded and

ran downstairs to the basement to get water. I returned to see that Connor had the whole situation under control and the crowd had meekly done as he'd asked. At last the plan went into operation: the customer bought a book, gave me their name, I wrote it on a Post-it note, Stephanie signed and they left happy. All the while, Connor stood by her table like a bodyguard, with Raffy at his feet.

'Good work, young man,' said Stephanie when, a couple of hours later, the last person had got their book signed and disappeared.

'Glad to be of assistance,' he said.

'You really helped today. Have you done this kind of work before?'

Even though it was Connor, I felt a flash of annoyance. I could see what was happening. He'd taken over and was going to be given my job!

'Not exactly,' Connor replied. 'But my parents are both secondary school teachers. I learnt how to do The Voice from them.'

Stephanie beamed at him. 'You do it well,' she said, then leant over to stroke Raffy.

Connor gave her his winning smile. 'They have a Look too, the one they use on the really young kids. The Don't-Push-It Look.'

I felt like giving him The Look.

'And can you do it?' asked Stephanie as she straightened back up.

Connor gave her a very stern look.

She cracked up. 'Scary,' she said. 'And do you work?'

Connor shook his head. 'Uni. I'm studying photography.'

'Really?' said Stephanie, then looked at me. 'Jess, can I have a word?' She drew me aside behind a bookshelf. I felt my heart sink as I prepared myself for a major telling-off.

When we were alone, she put her arm around me and gave me a squeeze. 'You were so right to call your friend and ask him to help out,' she said. 'Shows you have initiative.'

'I—'

'So, do you think he'd like to be part of the team?'

Ah, so she does want to give him my job, I thought. 'I'm so sorry,' I said. 'I realise I messed up this morning, but there was a queue in Fortnum's and this woman in front of me had got the wrong credit card—'

'Jess, what are you on about?'

'Being a rubbish PA and it's only my first day. I . . . I think Connor would probably love to be a part of your team, but I wish you'd give me another go too. I won't mess up again. Next time, I'd send someone else out to get the tea and wouldn't leave your side. Please don't sack me yet.'

'Sack you? I meant to have Connor along as well as you, not *instead* of. He said you were friends? He could help us with the queues as well as be the official tour photographer. He looks a nice young man, but I wouldn't want to employ someone if you're not OK with it too. I want Team Harper to be a happy team.'

The penny finally dropped. 'A . . . As *well as?*' I stuttered, then grinned. 'Hey, *yeah*.'

'So what do you think?' I asked Connor after I explained Stephanie's proposition.

'Wow. Unexpected,' he said. 'But then that's what my horoscope said for this week.' He grinned. 'I read Stephanie's online forecast this morning.'

'What sign are you?' I asked.

'Taurus, the bull,' he said. 'We're supposed to be stubborn, loyal, hedonistic – because we're ruled by Venus, the planet of love and beauty. What are you?'

'Sagittarian. Half man, half horse,' I said and made a neighing noise.

Connor cracked up. 'Seriously. I don't know much

about star signs but I read a bit last night online after your text. It's interesting. So what's your sign supposed to be like?'

'Sporty, which I am.'

'Which sport?'

'Swimming. I was on the school team last year and even won the championship, though lately with exams and stuff, I've hardly been near a swimming pool. Er, Sagittarius is a fire sign, so energetic. Can be clumsy. Say what we think even if it's inappropriate sometimes.'

'I like that,' said Connor. 'I like to know where I am with people. I can't be doing with people that have secrets and you have to prise what they're feeling out of them. My girlfriend, Naomi – I mean ex-girl-friend – was like that.'

I was about to ask more about his ex when Stephanie came over to join us. 'So have you decided if you're going to be part of our team, Connor?'

'It would be an honour, Ms Harper,' he said. 'Just one small problem.'

'And what's that?' asked Stephanie.

Connor looked down at Raffy.

'Ah,' said Stephanie. 'Can't you get someone to look after him?'

'Not all the time.'

Stephanie thought for a moment. 'Then bring him where you can. I love dogs. I have two back home and I miss them so much. It will be lovely to have some canine company.'

I burst out laughing. 'Bethany's going to love this,' I said. 'First a schoolgirl and now a dog on the team.'

'And the dog's master,' said Connor.

'My book tour,' said Stephanie. 'My entourage. Some people like to take a masseuse and a chef out on the road with them. I like to take a dog and two teenagers. I told you I'm an Aquarian. We always like to do things differently.'

Connor glanced at the schedule I'd handed him earlier and looked worried. 'It's a flight to Edinburgh later in the week. I couldn't bring Raffy there,' he said.

'No problem,' Stephanie said. 'Jess and I can do that one on our own, but most of the places on the tour will be journeys by car or train. So are you in?'

'I've just got to make a call,' said Connor. Stephanie nodded that he should go ahead so he took Raffy outside. I could see him talking to someone through the store window. Spending time on tour with Connor would be a great way to get to know him without having to commit to anything or feeling that I was getting into something too soon after JJ. Perfect. I didn't have to wait long to find out. He returned five minutes later with a grin on his face.

'I'm in,' he said and high-fived Stephanie and then me.

'Team Harper. It's a goer,' said Stephanie.

Before I went to sleep later that night, I sat at my computer to send my update to Bethany. I remembered what Stephanie had said earlier in the day about always putting a positive spin on things and chuckled to myself as I wrote. A hugely successful day. We sold over three hundred books. A very enthusiastic crowd came to meet Stephanie.

Very enthusiastic? The PR way of describing a mob, I thought.

Bethany must have been at her desk because she replied straightaway. Yes. I heard it was a good day. Stephanie has been in touch. Apparently two new team members, Connor and Raffy? Can you please explain who Raffy is and what experience he has had? Stephanie was a little vague.

I bet she was, I thought. *Now. How am I going to*

put a PR spin on the fact that the new team member is a dog?

I emailed back. Raffy has lots of experience in security. He is loyal and often described as the perfect travel companion. He will keep Stephanie safe.

Maybe when the tour was over, I'd send her a photo of Raffy – or even Skype her when Connor and Raffy were with me so we could introduce him and see her reaction. She'd probably have a fit.

Happiness is:
A job well done.
Learning new skills.
Surprise new friendships.
No communication from Keira.

Who am I?
Changing. Last week a cleaner. This week a celebrity's PA.

13

On the Road

The next day, Team Harper went to a library in North London where one of the local bookshops was supplying the books to be sold and a local radio station was coming to interview Stephanie. Connor met us there and brought his camera ready to photograph Stephanie with her fans. Outside, it was pouring with rain again so we raced from the car into the Victorian building. A middle-aged librarian with short black hair looked up from her computer at the desk to the right of the door. Her colour flushed red when she saw Raffy. She stood up and pointed at the door. 'Out,' she ordered. 'This is a LIBRARY! No dogs.'

Stephanie nodded at Connor and he and Raffy left immediately.

'Can I help you?' asked the lady, though she gave us a look as if to say that help was the last thing she wanted to do.

I told her who Stephanie was and why we were there. 'You are expecting us, aren't you? Ms Harper is scheduled to do a short talk, an interview and a signing.'

The librarian looked very harassed. 'Yes. No,' she said and pointed to a room at the back. 'Lesley was supposed to be in charge of this but she's not here. The bookshop people have already arrived, everything is being set up back there. Like I said, it was Lesley who organised it, so I don't know much about what's going on.'

'Will Lesley be here later?' asked Stephanie.

'She's on maternity leave,' said the lady and she stabbed her forefinger in the direction of a door at the back of the library. 'You go back there.'

As we made our way over, I looked for any signs of advertising but there wasn't a poster or leaflet about Stephanie's visit in sight.

Once inside the back room, a sweet young girl with frizzy ginger hair came forward. 'Ms Harper, I'm Izzie from the local bookshop. I'm so pleased to meet you,' she said and indicated a few rows of chairs she'd put out. 'I wasn't sure how many seats we'd need.'

'Hundreds if yesterday was anything to go by,' I said and looked round to see stacks of chairs at the back. 'I can help you put chairs out.'

Stephanie shook her head and put her hand on my arm. 'No. I've got a bad feeling about this. If there's no sign of anyone so far, I doubt if it's going to be a big turn-out, especially in this rain.'

'Do you know when the person from the radio station's coming?' I asked Izzie.

Izzie shook her head, shrugged and pointed at a table piled high with Stephanie's books. 'We just brought the books. The library was supposed to be in charge of everything else – the advertising and so on – but with Lesley away, it seems it's been overlooked. Um … I'll be over there if you need me.' And with that, she made a hasty retreat.

After sitting at the signing table for about ten minutes, Stephanie nudged me and looked at the door. 'Do you think we dare ask Ms Grump out there for a cup of coffee?'

I glanced at Izzie who was at the table with books and was busy texting. 'I'll go and find out,' I said.

I made my way back to the librarian in the main area. 'Excuse me, is there a café or kitchen anywhere nearby where I can get Ms Harper a drink?'

The lady looked annoyed. 'A *drink*? There's a small kitchen around the back. I suppose you can help yourself.'

'And we were wondering how many people to expect. Was the event advertised?'

'I *told* you, Lesley should have done it, I can't be expected to do her job as well as my own.'

'And you don't happen to know anything about the radio interview, do you?'

'I don't. It's Lesley's domain,' she said, then ran her fingers through her hair, sighed in an exasperated way and slumped back over her computer like she had all the cares of the world on her shoulders.

And no Lesley to help her out, I thought as I found the kitchen. I pulled my printed schedule out of my bag and looked to see if the mysterious Lesley's contact details were on there. They were so I quickly dialled her number. I got through to an answering machine so left a message explaining the situation. I tried Bethany's number too, in case she could help, but that went through to voicemail as well. I thought about making some tea but there were several old wet teabags dumped on the surface and the whole place looked like it needed a good clean. Luckily there was a small bottle of water in the fridge so I took that and went back to find Stephanie.

She stood up and came over to me. 'I think we should move on,' she whispered. 'I've had one enquiry – and that was from an elderly gentlemen who thought I worked here and wanted to know where the history section was. I have a feeling he's the only person we're going to see today.'

She went over to Izzie. 'I'm so sorry there won't be any sales, but I think it's best that you don't waste any more of your time here either.' She turned back to me. 'Come on, Jess. Team Harper are moving on.'

As we went back through to the main section of the library, Ms Grump looked surprised when we told her we were leaving. 'But what if the rain stops and someone turns up? What can I tell them? You can't leave. What if someone makes the effort to come out?'

Stephanie smiled sweetly. 'Now why would they do that? How would they even know I was here when there are no posters up? Please give anyone my apologies, but tell them when it comes to effort, I came all the way from the States to meet them.' She indicated that we should go.

The librarian made a sort of snorting noise and gave Stephanie a very disapproving look. 'Well! Some people.'

When we got outside, we joined Connor and Raffy who were standing under an umbrella near the car. Stephanie let out a long breath. 'She was some piece of work, hey? What a horrible atmosphere she created; it felt like quicksand in there, which is a shame because most libraries are full of atmosphere and great librarians who are more than eager to help. Let's go and get a coffee and a cake,' she said as the chauffeur got out of the car to open the door for her. 'Nearest cake shop, please. My team and I need a sugar hit.'

'Don't you mind?' I asked as I climbed into the car after her.

Stephanie shrugged. 'Some days I do but I could have predicted something like this would happen on a day when Mercury has gone retrograde.'

'What does that mean?' asked Connor as Raffy and he got into the front seat and the car pulled away. 'Mercury retrograde?'

'Mercury is the planet of communication,' Stephanie replied. 'When it goes retrograde, all sorts of mix-ups happen – miscommunications, that sort of thing.'

'I hope it's not still retrograde when my GCSE results come out,' I said.

'When's that?' asked Stephanie.

'August twenty-second.'

'It will be moving forward again by then so no communications mix-ups,' said Stephanie. 'Are you feeling anxious about them?'

'I'm trying not to think about them.'

'Very wise,' said Stephanie. 'People spend too much time worrying about things that never happen.'

'Do things always go wrong on retrograde days?' asked Connor.

Stephanie nodded. 'There's usually something. Like today, I half expected this so I was prepared, although sometimes it can be a waste of my time and folk don't appreciate that I've come a long way but ...' She shrugged. 'That's how it goes sometimes. You win some, you lose some. You just have to roll with the changes.'

'Doesn't it annoy you though?' asked Connor.

'It used to, and it definitely would if all the events

were like that, but they're not. Most of the people I meet have a real passion for books and reading. I look upon experiences like back there as a reality check, as if,' she pointed up to the sky, 'someone up there is saying, "Stephanie, you don't get above yourself now." You know the two mistakes you can make in life?'

Connor and I shook our heads.

'One is to think you're special,' said Stephanie. 'The other is to think that you're not.'

I laughed. 'I like that.'

'I still remember the days when I was nobody and hadn't two dimes to my name. I'm doing well now, but I know that fame is a fickle friend. One day you're up. One day you're down. One day you're in, one day you're out. One place I get treated as a celebrity, another day, someone like that lady back there looks at me as if to say, "Who do you think you are then?" And I have to ask myself the same question. Yeah, who *do* I think I am?'

'I've been asking myself that question too,' I told her. 'We're doing it as a project for school. Who am I?'

'A constantly changing being,' said Stephanie.

I grinned back at her. 'That's exactly what I wrote in my journal.'

'It's all an evolution,' Stephanie continued, 'and just as you think you know who you are, something comes along to change that perception. Just go with the flow, that's my motto, and try not to be too rigid about plans or how you want things to be or you'll just get worn out.' She smiled. 'Go with the ride and try not to resist where it takes you.'

Mum would have liked you, I thought. She'd often come out with stuff about life being a rollercoaster ride – up, down and round and round we go.

In the afternoon, the rollercoaster took us up, up, up. A big crowd was outside the bookshop in South London and they started waving madly as we drew up. The driver turned in to the car park where we saw a small group of people waiting. When we got out of the car, we noticed that all of them were wearing T-shirts with Stephanie's face on them.

A young lady with spiky blonde hair came forward. She gestured to the group around her. 'Welcome, Ms Harper. We're huge fans of yours and we've volunteered to be your entourage for the day,' she said. 'We'll escort you inside. I'm so thrilled to meet you.'

Stephanie looked back at me and winked as she

was taken inside the shop. The staff were warm and welcoming and one of them guided us to a table where there was a huge cake with all the symbols of the zodiac on top in pink icing and a bottle of pink champagne and glasses.

'You made this for me?' asked Stephanie, who looked touched by their efforts. 'Who's the chef?'

The girl with spiky hair put up her hand and blushed.

'Thank you so much, honey. I'm going to have me a big piece when we're done here.'

The girl flushed even pinker but looked really pleased.

The session was a huge success with loads of books sold and a perfectly behaved queue.

'I feel like a total hanger-on today. I've not had to do anything,' Connor said as we sat at the side, stuffing our faces with cake and sneaking pieces to Raffy as Stephanie chatted happily with her fans.

'No way,' I said. 'I've seen you taking your shots. With you along, we have a record of where we've been and who we've met.'

'I wish I could have got a shot of the woman this morning before she ordered me out,' he said. 'That was one grumpy lady!'

He then did a brilliant impersonation of the lady at the library, which made me almost spit cake crumbs out. Not a good look when you're trying to look cool, but Connor didn't seem to mind. I think he enjoyed making me laugh and I got the impression that Stephanie liked having him along too. We really were Team Harper and when I emailed Bethany later that night, I could say truthfully that we were a happy team out on the road. I didn't mention the grumpy lady and disaster in the morning. Instead, I concentrated on the success of the afternoon. In the car on the way home, Stephanie had told me that good PR meant highlighting the positive. I decided to apply that way of thinking to my life and Keira as well as my reports back to Bethany.

<u>Who am I?</u>
Someone who's learning to roll with the changes. This week I have been part of Team Harper, last week I was a cleaner, the week before a babysitter, before that a schoolgirl, next week who knows? But those roles are not who I am. Who I am is the person who takes on those roles. (Oo-er, I've come over all deep.)

14

Keira's Campaign Continues

The next week was a blur of bookshops, booksellers and queues of Stephanie's fans. We hit the motorway some of the time, another day we took the train and travelled up as far as the Midlands, Birmingham and Nottingham. A montage of snapshot images of the tour stayed in my head. Like standing on a train station platform which was warm one minute and then a wind whipped up, blowing Stephanie's paper out of her hands, followed by a fast and furious downpour of hail. None of us had jackets on that were warm enough. Another day, our train was delayed and we all had to race up and down stairs and along platforms to catch our connection, which we made by seconds. Raffy thought it was a game and seemed to be enjoying it immensely. Part of the montage were moments with Connor. His easy smile, twinkling eyes and a few times when Stephanie was occupied elsewhere and it was just him and me, sharing a sandwich or cup of tea. Even though I'd only known him such a short time, I felt comfortable with him like I'd known him for ages.

Then there were the early mornings, the hair-dryer blasting, then applying make-up to my bleary face. Late nights trying to find somewhere to grab a cup of coffee – one time Connor tried to get a café to stay open telling them that *the* Stephanie Harper was outside. 'Tell her she could be the Queen of Sheba and we'd still be closed,' replied the café assistant. To drive her point home, she tried to mop him out of the place as if he was a piece of dirt on her floor.

There were a few miscommunications about places and times, one signal failure that caused a delay, and one signing went on over time, but somehow we managed to make it to all of Stephanie's events. It was always lovely to see her fans – small groups, larger groups – all eager to see Stephanie, the astrology queen.

Witnessing her amazing calm and energy made me realise just how hard she worked and that it wasn't all glamour and swanning in and out of places. There was no time off and each day brought a new challenge – if not the weather then a travel problem or a bookshop that wasn't as with it as the others. Each signing and event was different, but Stephanie always seemed to have an explanation for everything that happened: it was all according to the stars – either Pluto sextile with Mars caused this or Saturn conjunct with the sun was responsible for that. It was still like listening to a foreign language for me, but the basics were beginning to sink in.

I was really enjoying travelling around and being part of Team Harper – especially as I was getting to know Connor better. I liked the way he was with people, charming but in charge. I felt safe with him around and he often made some flirtatious comment to spice the day up a little.

The only sour note for me was that Keira was continuing her 'I hate Jess' campaign. When I got home in the evening, I always checked my computer to see if Alisha or JJ were online to say hello over Skype, or to see if Charlie had sent me an email to update me on his holiday.

Some nights when I went online, I would find a private message on my Facebook from Keira or a nasty note from her on my wall for all my friends to see. I always deleted the wall messages straight away, but by then the damage had already been done. I was at a loss as to what to do about it. I kept planning to report her but I kept hoping that she'd get bored and just go away.

One evening there was a message on my wall saying, *Princess Perfect is off in her limo again.* It gave me the creeps because it sounded as if she was watching my movements from somewhere. Pia told me to take no notice, repeating that Kiera was just a nutter and any response from me would only encourage her more.

During the day, when I was busy on the tour, I did manage to put thoughts about Kiera aside, but at night, when I was going to sleep, the things she'd written played over and over in my head and I felt frustrated at not being able to stop her. I also wondered who was reading what she wrote and if they thought that it was true – I was friends with a lot of people on Facebook and some of them didn't know me that well.

Quite a few friends had written comments supporting me under her postings, messages like, *Get a life*, and *Leave Jess alone whoever you are*. Pia had written, *Keira is a sad loser*, under the text about me being Princess Perfect. I hoped that Keira saw the messages of support before I deleted each conversation with her post and the comments after it. I was grateful for the support, but I couldn't help it; Keira was getting to me again and getting under my skin, which really annoyed me. I'd make up replies, what I'd like to say to her in my defence, and often didn't get to sleep until the early hours of the morning. *Why don't you like me? What have I ever done to you? We used to be friends once. What changed? Why me? Why? Why?*

On the Friday evening, I got home to see that Kiera had posted on my wall again and uploaded another old photo from my childhood. One where I was pulling a face to camera. I remembered the day, we'd been larking about doing our worst face possible. It was supposed to have been for a laugh, not to use as ammunition when we were older. Underneath it, she'd written: *Princess Perfect isn't so perfect*.

I felt like posting underneath, *Why, Keira?* but I reminded myself, not to engage. That's what she'd want.

That night, I made a promise to myself not to look at Facebook any more but I knew that another part of me couldn't help it. A side of me had to know if she'd been on there and what she was saying about me.

I called Pia for our regular catch-up.

'I could always delete my page,' I suggested.

'You could,' Pia agreed, 'but then she'll have won, won't she? Why should you? Just keep deleting her posts, then ignore her and she'll get bored and move on.'

I wish I shared Pia's conviction, I thought as I got into bed later and attempted to get to sleep.

'Are some star signs more prone to bullying?' I asked Stephanie the next day as we drove up to North London to pick up Connor and Raffy.

'No, not really,' she said. 'Someone being a bully is more to do with what a person has experienced in life. Sometimes they've been bullied themselves.' She looked at me closely. 'Why do you ask?'

I looked out of the window and tried to appear casual. 'Oh, no reason.'

'What's going on, Jess? Is someone bullying you?'

My casual act disintegrated and my eyes welled up with tears.

Stephanie immediately reached over and put her hand over mine. 'Hey, honey, what's been going on?'

She was looking at me with such kindness, the way Mum used to look at me when I was poorly or upset, and before I could help myself, I'd poured the whole story out to her.

Stephanie put her arm around me and gave me a hug. 'Have you told your dad?'

I shook my head. 'We're like ships that pass in the night,' I said. 'And he has a lot on his plate with looking after Porchester Park.'

'I'm sure he'd want to know that you've been hurting.'

That made me cry again. I sniffed back my tears. 'Sorry. Not sure what's the matter with me. I don't usually cry.'

Stephanie pointed at the sky. 'Full moon in Cancer. The moon rules water. We're more than sixty per cent water. Most people get a bit emotional when there's a full moon, even more so when it's in Cancer.' She handed me a tissue. 'More often than not, bullies are cowards. This Keira has to be stopped. Do you know where she lives?'

I nodded. 'But I don't want to see her. My friend

Pia says not to engage or respond because that's what she wants. To see that she's got to me.'

'Pia's right. But surely she has parents? Maybe your dad could talk to them?'

I let out a moan.

Stephanie nodded. 'Sorry. No, course not. That would make her even more mad.'

'Exactly.'

Our conversation was cut short when the driver slowed down and pulled over to pick up Connor.

'Please don't say anything to him, will you?' I asked Stephanie.

'Course not, but we are going to resume this later, OK?'

I nodded, wiped my eyes and put my happy face on for Connor. I didn't want him to know about Keira or see me in Blub City.

Every evening, Pia came over to help me pick outfits for the next day and catch up on our days as working girls.

'Once this is all over, we should plan a really good week off,' she said. 'Us time.'

I nodded but I knew that Pia was as happy as I was

now Henry had returned to England and they were working together at Porchester Park.

'How you getting on with Stephanie?' she asked as she sat back on my bed.

'I'm getting to know her better,' I replied as I painted my nails a deep raspberry colour.

'How does she know the Lewis family?'

'She was at university with Mrs Lewis. "Roomies" as Stephanie says. She told me they were a pair of hippies, with her into astrology and Mrs Lewis wanting to save the world. Apparently, Mrs Lewis was always going on protests and almost getting arrested.'

Pia laughed. 'Hard to imagine that, isn't it?'

I nodded. 'But I really like the fact that they're still best mates. I hope we'll stay friends forever.'

Pia pulled a sad face. 'Not much chance of that, Jess. I've been meaning to tell you for a while now. I don't like you any more, in fact, I never did.'

I picked up a cushion and biffed her with it. 'Me too. I don't like you either.'

Pia biffed me back. 'You know we'll be mates for ever, *stupoid*. Is she married?'

'Stephanie? She was. Divorced. They have their son so she stays in touch with her ex.'

'Do you like her?' said Pia.

'Oh yes. She makes me laugh because she has an explanation for everything. Feeling emotional? Moon in Cancer. Post not arriving? Mercury is retrograde.'

'Why would that affect the post?'

'Mercury is the planet that rules communication. If it goes retrograde—'

'Your post goes with it.'

I nodded. 'Something like that. I think she likes having Connor, Raffy and me along, though – sort of a make-do family in her son's absence. She said it's lonely being out on the road so it's good to have someone along to talk to and share it all with. I get the impression that she wishes her son was with her, though.'

'He'll be the one I showed you in the photo on the net. Kind of geeky but cute. Where is he? Back in the States?'

'No. He's on a gap year. His name's Dylan. He was in Thailand, but the last thing she heard he was travelling around Europe. Stephanie really misses him and is hoping that he'll come over to the UK while she's here.'

'Why doesn't he?'

I shrugged. 'She said he's always been a free spirit. Goes where he likes, when he likes and gets in touch when he likes. She wishes he'd contact her more. She worries about him.'

'How old is he?'

'Nineteen, I think.'

'Maybe you'll meet him one day.'

I knew what she was thinking. 'Pia, stop match-making me with boys you don't even know. The last thing I'd need would be another boy who travels a lot.'

'OK. I just want you to know that there is life after JJ. So, back to boys in the UK. What's happening with Connor?' asked Pia. 'Any progress?'

'He's very flirty but not just with me. He's Mr Charm with Stephanie and all her fans too. Stephanie says he has Libra rising, which makes him a natural charmer.'

'What does she mean, "Libra rising"?'

'Everyone has a rising sign as well as a star sign. There are twelve star signs, right?'

Pia nodded. 'And that's down to when in the month you were born, yeah?'

'Yes. But it's so much more complicated than that. We are affected by all the planets apparently, ten of them,' I said. 'So your star sign depends on where the sun was when you were born.'

'Star sign, sun sign? Now you're confusing me.'

'Your star sign is sort of the same as your sun sign; it's just another way of saying it.'

' And how come ten planets?' asked Pia. 'You just said there are twelve star signs or sun signs or whatever they are.'

'Mercury rules two star signs, er ... Gemini and Virgo and Venus also rules two and they are Libra and Taurus.'

'Astrology swot,' said Pia. She sighed. 'Sounds way too complicated for me. I just like to read my horoscope in a magazine, end of.'

'It's quite a science once you get into it. I've been reading up on it on the tour, plus Stephanie has explained some to me. The month you're born in determines what sun or star sign you are, but the rising sign changes every two hours and, er ... I can't quite remember how often the other ones change. We're affected by the position of the other planets too.'

'OK, let's see if you know all twelve signs and their planets, I bet you don't.'

'Aries is ruled by Mars, Taurus by Venus, Gemini by Mercury, Cancer by the moon, Leo the sun. Virgo by Mercury, Libra by Venus, Scorpio by Pluto, Sagittarius by Jupiter, Capricorn by Saturn, Aquarius by Uranus and Pisces by Neptune.'

Pia sank to her knees, put her arms in the air and bowed. 'I'm not worthy,' she said, then got back up. 'Wow, you've really been taking it in.'

I nodded. I was surprised by how much I'd picked up from Stephanie and how quickly I could list the signs and planets for Pia. 'Plus everyone is affected by the time they are born and the location.' I added, 'So that explains why you can have two people both born under the sun sign of Pisces but they seem quite different. Depending on what time of the day and place they are born, they will have different rising signs. Do you see?'

Pia nodded. 'No,' she said with a grin.

'If you're born on January twenty-third at four o'clock in the morning, you'd be Aquarius with, say, Sagittarius rising. Someone born two hours later would also be Aquarius but have Scorpio rising. Get it?'

Pia laughed. 'Sort of. So although I am an Aries, and have Mars as my ruling planet, I have a different rising sign to Aries?'

'Yes. There are loads of websites that work it out for you for free. You just have to put in your date of birth, time of birth and place. I'll get you a copy of Stephanie's book and you can read about it for yourself. It's actually really interesting and can tell you loads about people. For example, Connor is Taurus with Libra rising and his moon is in Pisces, which makes him a bit of a flirt but underneath all that, he's a softie.'

'Moon in Pisces?'

'Yes. Where your moon is affects how you are emotionally. The moon changes signs every two days.'

'Information overload. Forget about the science of astrology for a moment,' said Pia. 'What about *chemistry* between you and Connor? Is there any?'

'I think so,' I replied. 'I definitely get a vibe that he likes me, though he does talk about his ex a lot.'

'In a good or bad way?'

'He's not horrible about her, but he gets a look when he talks about her – kind of sad and closed-in at the same time. I think whatever happened between them hurt him. I get the feeling there is some unresolved stuff with her.'

'Hmm,' said Pia. 'Hope he's not on the rebound. Sometimes when boys have just broken up with someone, they seem to think they have to prove that they're still attractive and start a relationship up really quickly just to show that they're still in the game. Maybe you need to be careful.'

Pia's words struck a chord with me and not just about Connor. I wondered if part of my attraction to him was because *I* was on the rebound after JJ and felt I had to prove to myself that I didn't need him by getting off with another attractive boy.

'Maybe. He did say that his relationship with her was a closed chapter, though, and one he wouldn't be revisiting.'

Pia frowned. 'Just be careful, Jess. You don't want to be his counsellor.'

'I'll see what happens. I'm not going to rush into anything.'

Pia shot me one of her 'I don't believe you' looks.

'Seriously,' I said. I missed JJ a lot and it still hurt that I didn't know if or when I would ever see him again.

'Sure,' she replied and she glanced at my nails and the clothes we'd laid out for tomorrow. 'Which is why you don't care what you wear each day.'

I biffed her with a pillow again. Having a best mate who knows me so well means no secrets. I did like Connor. I liked him a *lot*. The more time we spent together, the more he grew on me, but he hadn't made a move nor had I encouraged him too much. There was just a bit of flirting and banter, but no more than that. I think Raffy had more of a crush on me than Connor. It was another reason I was being quite cool with him, apart from still missing JJ; I didn't want to get my feelings trodden on in case Connor didn't want any more than for us to be good friends.

'Have you told him about JJ?'

I shook my head.

'Why not?' asked Pia. 'He's told you about his ex.'

I shrugged. 'Only a bit about her. I'm not sure why I haven't mentioned JJ. Partly because it's never seemed like the right time and partly because JJ isn't exactly an ex in the same way that Connor's girlfriend is.'

'JJ wants you to be happy, Jess,' said Pia. 'He said he didn't want to hold you back.'

'I know. Still it's early days, isn't it?'

'Maybe the stars will work it out for you,' said Pia. 'Which one governs love?'

'Venus.'

'So when Venus is in the right place, perhaps everything will become clear.'

'Maybe, but it would have to be the same in Connor's chart,' I said.

'Or maybe you just get him behind a bookshelf one day and snog him,' said Pia. 'Sometimes you just have to go for it.'

'You would say that,' I said, 'you being an Aries.'

Pia rolled her eyes. 'Oh hark at you, the new astrology queen.'

Happiness is:
A sense of new possibilities.

Unhappiness is:
Being the target of someone's
nastiness.

15

Scotland the Brave

—

Stephanie and I got an early flight to Edinburgh on Sunday. Connor didn't come with us because he couldn't find anyone to look after Raffy.

The flight from London was fine but the traffic from the airport to the centre of town was really bad. I'd checked the schedule before we set off and knew that we were due at a big bookshop in the centre of town at midday.

'The bookshop on Princes Street?' asked the taxi driver.

'Yes, thanks,' I replied as I checked my watch. If he got a move on, we might just make it.

But when we arrived at the shop, it was clear that the staff weren't expecting us.

'Are you sure you're meant to be here?' asked one of the sales assistants – Lucy, a sweet girl with a round face and big blue eyes.

I got out my schedule again. Maybe we'd got the wrong day or week. 'Yes, it definitely says today,' I said as I glanced over the page.

'Oh, wait, you do know that there are two book-shops on this street?' said Lucy and pointed out the door. We followed her to look out on to the busy street. 'The other one is right down at the other end of this road.'

Oh no, I thought as Stephanie checked her watch.

'It's midday now. If we get a taxi, we'll only be a bit late,' she said.

We all ran out onto the pavement and looked for a taxi. I couldn't see one and even if there had been an empty one, I could see that the traffic was at a standstill due to the roadworks that had caused delays earlier.

'How far?' I asked Lucy.

'Ten minutes if you run,' she replied. 'I'm sorry, I only have my bike so I can't give you a lift.'

I glanced at Stephanie.

'I'm game if you are,' she said.

We pelted off at full speed down the road and finally could see the second bookshop – I just hoped it was the right one this time.

'Just a sec,' said Stephanie. 'I have to catch my breath.'

We stopped for a while and waited until we'd stopped panting. Stephanie started laughing. 'Bet you never imagined this when you took the job,' she said.

I shook my head. 'Not exactly. I'm so sorry, I should have checked.'

Stephanie waved a hand as if dismissing what I was saying. 'Not your fault. You weren't to know. Anyway, you know my mottos by now – each day brings a new challenge? You can either freak out or flow with it.'

I laughed. I really liked her attitude to life. She wasn't at all diva-like. She smoothed her hair and walked into the shop, cool as a cucumber, as if she'd just stepped out of an air-conditioned limo. She was such a pro.

There were loads of people waiting inside and they cheered when they saw Stephanie. She apologised for the delay then got stuck in to the signing. It was a great turn-out with around three hundred people in the queue, so the next few hours flew past. When it finally looked like it was winding down, I noticed a blond boy hovering in the shadows of the shelves. When Stephanie was engaged in talking to one of her fans, the boy beckoned me towards him. He was tall and tanned with little round glasses and had a red paisley scarf knotted over his head. He had the look of someone who had been travelling. As I went over, I thought that he looked vaguely familiar.

He pulled me out of sight behind the shelves and I was about to protest when I realised where I knew his face from.

'Hey, you're Dylan, Stephanie's son.'

He flashed me a smile. 'I am. And you must be Jess.'

'How did you know?'

He tapped his nose. 'Bethany. I asked her where Mom was. She told me where she'd be today and that you were accompanying her.'

'Your mum is going to be so pleased to see you.'

'Hope so. I wanted to surprise her.'

'Come on out, then. She's almost finished.'

Dylan held back. 'I'll wait a moment till she's really finished. I know my mom at these events. There's always another person to talk to on the way out.'

I nodded. It was true. Stephanie was very generous with her time.

Dylan grinned. 'Hey, I'm supposed to spy on you,' he said.

'Spy? For who?'

'Bethany, of course.'

'You'd make a rubbish spy, then,' I said. 'You're supposed to keep the mission secret.'

Dylan cracked up. 'I can see why Mom hired you. I can report back favourably back to Bethany.'

'But you've only just met me.'

He stood back and gave me another long look. 'I go by instinct and you look OK.'

I laughed. He had a nice open face and I thought he looked OK too. Not in a fancying him kind of way, but like he'd be an interesting person to get to know. 'You're like your mum, then. She goes by what she feels too. Are you staying in Scotland? What are your plans?'

'I don't usually do plans. Let it flow, that's my motto.'

'That's one of your mum's too.'

He smiled again. 'You don't grow up in a house with someone like her without some of that "go with your heart and let the universe speak to you" stuff rubbing off. So plans, yeah, I thought I'd come and catch up with Mom then see how it goes. But I might come back to London for a while.'

'Cool. She'll like that.'

I glanced at Stephanie who looked like she had finished. 'Shall I let her know you're here?'

Dylan nodded so I went over to Stephanie. 'I have one last person who wants to have a word,' I said.

Stephanie sighed and looked at her watch. 'We ought to be getting back to the airport,' she said.

'I think you might want to see this person,' I said. 'He's over by the shelf to your left.'

Stephanie glanced up and her face lit up when she saw Dylan step out. I felt a real tug in my heart as he gave his mum a huge hug and my eyes filled with tears. I would give anything to see my mum one more time. I brushed my tears away as Stephanie introduced us, then realised that we'd just met.

'But we have to go soon,' I told them. 'We have a flight booked back to London.'

'I'll come with you in the car to the airport,' said Dylan.

'Can't you come back to London with us?' asked Stephanie.

Dylan shook his head. 'I want to have a look around while I'm up here but I promise I'll visit you in London some time.'

On the flight back, Stephanie was quieter than

usual. I didn't disturb her because I could see that she was sad to have seen Dylan for such a short time, then to have left him in Scotland.

When we got into the limo taking us back to Porchester Park, she got out her laptop.

'I'm going to Skype the US,' she said.

'You can do that from a car?' I asked.

She nodded and turned on her machine. 'Yes, it has wi-fi, didn't you know?' Moments later, she had Skyped Mrs Lewis. They chatted for a while and I heard her say something about Dylan always doing his own thing, how she'd been just the same at his age and how he'd been a free spirit since he came out as gay when he was sixteen. I smiled to myself. So much for Pia plotting a love affair between us when she'd seen his picture online. That so wasn't going to happen. I looked out of the window and reflected on the day. It had been fun meeting Dylan.

Stephanie nudged me. 'Someone wants to say hello,' she said.

I glanced at her screen expecting to see Mrs Lewis and my heart skipped a beat when I saw it was JJ.

'Ohmigod! I was just thinking about you,' I said.

'And here I am,' he said.

'Unbelievable,' I said. 'I'm in a car!'

JJ laughed. He looked better than he had in recent days, more rested and like his old self as he chatted away. It felt so sophisticated to be gliding through the streets of London and talking to someone on the other side of the world. We chatted for a while and I told him a bit about the tour but I didn't say anything about how much I'd been missing him because I was aware that Stephanie was sitting beside me and felt a little shy of talking about feelings in front of her.

'I'm glad to hear you're happy and have been busy,' said JJ. 'And remember what I said in our last conversation?'

I nodded.

'Don't let anything hold you back,' he said. 'I meant what I said.'

I wondered if Stephanie had mentioned to Mrs Lewis that Connor was travelling with us and she had maybe passed that on to JJ. 'You too,' I said, although it hurt to say it. The thought of JJ with someone else was too painful but maybe he had met someone over in the States. If he had, I didn't want to know.

As we drew up outside Porchester Park, I said goodbye to JJ and felt sad. It was good to talk to him but it had also reminded me of the reality that we were in different countries with no idea if we might ever see each other again apart from in cyberspace.

'See you soon,' said Stephanie as she gathered her things. 'And thanks for your company today.'

She leant towards me to give me a hug. As I hugged her back, I noticed a group of girls on the other side of the street and my mood changed in a second. Keira was standing in a doorway with two other girls. She put her index and middle finger up to her eyes then pointed the same fingers at me, as if to say, 'I'm watching you'.

I turned away quickly. As Stephanie went inside, Yoram came over to me.

'You know those girls?' he asked me. He didn't look in Keira's direction but I knew he was talking about Keira and her companions.

'Sort of. I wish I didn't,' I said.

Yoram nodded. 'I've seen her hanging about here a few times lately,' he said. As always, his expression gave little away and I hoped that he wasn't notching Keira and her mates as another thing to add to his disapproval list about me.

'She's not a friend,' I said, to make it clear that I didn't want her around Porchester Park any more than he did.

With a gentle shove, Yoram pushed me towards the side entrance. 'You go on in.'

When I got home, I went straight up to my room to send Bethany an update on the day.

I wrote: A wonderful visit to Edinburgh today where we managed to fit in visits to two bookshops instead of one.

I smiled as I shut my computer. She didn't need to know that one of the bookshops was a total mistake!

Happiness is:
Talking on Skype to someone you care about (especially when doing it in the back of a limo!).

16

Connor

The time out on tour had flown by so fast and Edinburgh was the last stop. However, my job wasn't over yet because although the travelling part of the tour was done, Stephanie wanted to employ Connor and I for a few more days to write up the highlights of our trips so that she could post them on her blog and Facebook page along with some of the photos that Connor had taken. I was very happy about this because it meant that I could spend more time with Connor. After my conversation with JJ, I felt I needed some cheering up and reassurance that life could go on without him. All through the week on the road,

I'd felt that something was starting to happen between Connor and I. I'd often caught him looking at me and, the last time, he didn't look away and neither did I. Being on the rebound for either of us or not, it was a totally delicious sensation that went right down to my toes. I know he felt it too because he smiled and raised an eyebrow as if to say, 'Yeah, me too'.

He arrived for our first meeting with his camera which I connected up to my laptop on the breakfast bar in our kitchen, living area. We'd already agreed that Connor wouldn't bring Raffy to the house in case Dave freaked out – he didn't like dogs, especially not in his inner sanctum – so Connor left Raffy with Pia who took him for a walk with Henry in Hyde Park. Sorted. Everyone happy.

The plan was to go through all the shots that Connor had taken in the various places we'd been, so once everything was set up, we hopped onto the stools by the bar and he scrolled through the photos. It was then that I noticed he'd also taken some shots of me. Really fabulous shots.

'What do you think?' he asked as we both bent over to look.

'You've made me look really good,' I said.

'Only captured what's there,' he said, turning away from the screen and looking into my eyes.

I held his gaze and could feel the heat between us. The intensity of it made me blush. He had beautiful eyes, the colour of dark honey. Not taking his eyes away, he took my hand, then leant towards me. I moved towards him and our lips met. I reached up to put my hand on the back of his head when there was a noise at the front door. Someone was coming in. Thinking that it would be my dad, we both leapt apart.

'Charlie!' I said when I saw who it was.

He looked quizzically at Connor and gave him a nod to say hi. Typical Charlie. He's so laid-back, I could be sitting with a gorilla and he wouldn't question it. 'Hey, sis,' he said and came over to give me a hug. He looked fabulous, relaxed and happy with sun-kissed hair and a great tan. I introduced him to Connor and we spent the next fifteen minutes catching up, drinking coffees and, in Charlie's case, eating a huge cheese sandwich. I was so glad to hear that he'd had a great time and, as I'd known he would, had experienced a world full of luxury, not that Charlie was the least bit bothered about the linen he slept in or the standard of five-star accommodation. What he'd enjoyed was the sports, swimming, hiking and just hanging out with his mates.

When Charlie went upstairs to unpack, Connor and I went back to the laptop. He glanced over at me and gave me a cheeky grin. 'I suppose we'd better get on, hadn't we?'

I nodded. We were there to work, not have a snogging session, but I took his hand and squeezed it to let him know that I was happy to pick up later where we'd left off.

We decided to send five photographs of Stephanie to her for approval, then we set about writing up the highlights of the trip.

'Hey, you're good at this,' said Connor when he saw the piece I'd written about the Edinburgh trip.

'Thanks. Actually this whole experience has made me think about writing, you know, doing it at university.'

'What kind of writing? Journalism?'

'Oh. I don't know yet. I just know I like writing. Putting together the words.'

'I thought about writing for a while myself before I settled on photography. One of the hardest decisions about writing can be working out where you fit, like detective stories or sci-fi? Literary or commercial? Poetry or writing for TV? Magazines or newspapers? The list is endless, and then you have to decide who you want to write for – kids, adults, teenagers ...'

'Wow, yeah. I guess so. I hadn't thought of all that. Maybe I'll look into creative writing classes so that I can try a bit of everything and see what I like best.'

'You might find that you'd like to write the kind of thing you like to read,' he said. 'Do you like real-life books or fantasy?'

'A bit of both. But the idea of writing for a living is the first thing that's given me any kind of buzz, if you know what I mean.'

Connor nodded again. 'That's how I feel about photography. I love it and learning everything I can.'

It felt good to work and chat with Connor. It was so easy being with him. The other thing I liked was that he was from my world. Even though it hadn't ever been a problem with JJ, I couldn't help but wonder whether, in time, the differences in our lifestyles would have come between us.

When we'd finished our work, we made a date for the next day to meet up in Highgate near where

Connor lived. 'So we can walk Raffy,' he said, but I got the feeling it was also so we could be away from brothers and fathers and security men. He arranged to pick up Raffy from Pia and Henry at the park, so I walked him to the side gate that led out of Porchester Park and punched in the security number to let him out.

'You like living here?' he asked as the gate slowly began to open.

I shrugged. 'It's different. The apartments are stunning, I wish I could show you them. The rooms are as big as tennis courts and some of them have amazing works of art, like, the real thing, a real Picasso, not a poster.' I knew I shouldn't really be talking about private details, Dad had drummed it into me enough times, but I knew I could trust Connor.

'Would you live here if you had the money?' he said, then laughed. 'Oh, but you *do* live here. You know what I mean.'

'No way. I'd buy somewhere in Cornwall or somewhere with trees,' I said.

Connor laughed. 'Yeah, me too.'

He gave me a light kiss, then went through the gate. 'See you tomorrow,' he said. Three words but they were loaded.

'Later,' I said with a grin and went back in to find Charlie had come downstairs.

'So, what's going on there then?' he said.

'What do you mean?'

'Connor.'

I grinned. 'Early days. Nothing's really happened between us.'

I updated him on the JJ situation and that he would no longer be studying in the UK so felt it would be unfair to tie me down to any commitment. Charlie shrugged and said, 'Bummer.' I knew I wouldn't get much more out of him. He never said much when it came to talking about relationships so I moved on, told him more about the tour and showed him some of the pictures.

He glanced over them politely, but I could tell he wasn't really concentrating and soon he got up and put his jacket on. He wanted to go over to see Flo. 'By the way, I saw Keira out front when I arrived home,' he said. 'She's not been giving you a hard time, has she?'

I felt a shiver and wondered just how often she was out there watching my movements. 'She's been sending nasty messages again, but I try to ignore them. I don't like the idea of her hanging about, though. What do you think she wants?'

'She wants to get a life, that's what. Have you told Dad? Hanging about outside where we live is weird, even for her.'

'I haven't told him. I've been really busy and he always is, but I'll think about it,' I said. 'Best rule is don't engage with nutters, though, don't you think?'

He shrugged. 'I guess. But let me know if there's anything I can do.'

'Will do.'

Dad came home a few moments later to greet Charlie and I sat and listened as they had their catch-up. I wondered if this was the moment to tell him about Keira.

'Jess has been fantastic,' he told Charlie. 'She's worked very hard both here at Porchester Park and then for Stephanie. My two wonderful children. I'm so proud of both of you and the way you've interacted with the residents since you got here, as friends with some of them and Jess working as a member of staff and then for Stephanie. You have done Porchester Park proud.'

This was not a moment to ruin by telling him that actually a nutjob was hanging around outside. Maybe another time but my feeling was that it was *my* problem and I wanted to deal with it on my own.

When they'd gone, I thought back to the kiss with Connor. I never expected to feel anything so strongly so soon after JJ leaving but there was no denying it. There was something very special there. If it wasn't for Keira, life would be almost perfect.

17

Falling . . .

The following week with Connor was the sweetest. When I went up to meet him in Highgate as we'd planned at my house, we walked Raffy in the woods nearby and Connor kissed me again. It felt every bit as delicious and toe-curling as it had in our kitchen. He could make me melt by just looking into my eyes and holding my gaze. I loved hanging out with him, listening to him talk about his life and his uni course. I loved his slow smile and how he laughed often, a laugh that came right from his belly. I did feel a twinge of guilt in the beginning – it seemed so soon after JJ to be falling for another boy – but I reminded myself that JJ was on the other side of the world and had said he didn't want to hold me back.

Being with Connor felt like the perfect antidote to all the sadness about losing JJ and the anxiety Keira had caused with her nastiness over the summer. When I was with Connor, none of it seemed to matter and so I pushed my inner critic to the back of my mind and let myself surrender to what was happening between us.

Over the next weeks, we saw each other just about every day and I couldn't help but enjoy having a normal relationship, doing the sort of things most teenagers do – a walk in the park, sitting outside a café watching the world go by, going to see a movie then getting a pizza, holding hands and kissing as the sun went down over the Heath. Ordinary stuff that I hadn't always been able to do with JJ, but it never felt boring because I was with Connor and each day we spent together got better and better.

Dad would approve, I thought. *Me not hankering after the five-star world of Porchester Park.* Though sometimes I felt that Dad didn't totally get me. I reckoned I was always more realistic about hanging out with the Lewises than he gave me credit for. Of course I'd enjoyed the glimpse I'd had of their world – what normal teenage girl wouldn't – but it wasn't only the designer lifestyle I'd enjoyed. I'd genuinely liked Alisha and JJ and our friendship would have been the same, dosh or no dosh. Plus it had made me realise that you pay a price if you have a rich and famous parent. Although JJ's world was luxurious and A-list all the way, at times it had felt pressurised and claustrophobic; there was always a minder a short distance away when JJ or Alisha went out anywhere, and JJ and I had needed to sneak away if we wanted any time alone. I knew JJ longed for freedom. His dream afternoon would be to walk around London with a mate or by himself and not have to answer to anyone. Connor and I had so much more independence. OK, I had to tell Dad where I was going, but he was cool with it. He'd met Connor and liked him, though I hadn't told him that we were becoming more than workmates.

JJ and I still Skyped and texted regularly but I felt that there was more than just the distance of miles between us as I got increasingly involved with Connor. Despite promising to myself that I'd tell JJ what was going on, each call ended and I hadn't even broached the subject.

Still early days, I told myself, *and for all I know, JJ's starting seeing a girl over in the States. Plus,* I kept reminding myself, *it was him that suggested that we should both be free to date other people. Later,* I always told myself, *I'll tell him later. When his grandfather's better.*

'Seems you're officially an item,' said Flo as she sprawled back on one of the beanbags on the floor in the chill-out shed at the bottom of our garden.

Meg and Flo were back from their holidays and had come over to my house after we'd got our GCSE results. We were over the moon because all of us had done better than we'd thought we would. I'd got six A stars, one A and one B. Pia had got four A stars, three A's and two B's and Meg and Flo's results weren't far behind us. Connor had popped in to say congratulations and meet the girls but he didn't hang around as I think he knew it was girl time and we all had a lot of catching up to do as well as celebrate our good news.

After he'd left, I'd asked Meg and Flo what they thought. I searched their faces to see if they disapproved. 'I know it seems a bit fast after JJ . . .' I started.

Meg flicked her hand as if dismissing what I was saying. 'You do seem well-suited. I just want to see you happy and I'm sure so would JJ.'

more comfortable. I'd finally had space to enjoy some proper lie-ins and time to hang out with mates or Connor and I'd relished every second. It seemed natural to behave like a couple with Connor. He'd held my hand wherever we went, texted me when we weren't together, and when we were together, there was a lovely light feeling of walking on air. And it wasn't just the great snog sessions we had, Connor was really easy to talk to and found myself opening up to him in the same way I'd been able to with JJ.

The evening after Connor had met the girls, I went up to Highgate to see him. As we sat out in his back garden, I opened up to him even more, telling him about my mum, her illness and then later, her death and funeral. Connor was so kind and sympathetic, I couldn't hold back the tears and he held me in his arms until they subsided. I thought about my mum every single day and still found myself wanting to tell her things or ask her opinion, only to realise that she'd gone and could no longer be reached. In turn, Connor told me about losing his elder brother in a car accident when he was seven. His brother was nine. His face flushed red with anger and grief as he told me his story and this time, I held him. I felt so close to him, like I could tell him anything and he would be there for me. I decided it was time to tell him about JJ so there were no secrets between us.

He listened without interrupting but took my hand and held it as I told him what had happened. 'You really liked this guy, huh?' he asked when I'd finished.

I nodded. 'Sometimes it just doesn't work out. Bad timing, whatever, sometimes life conspires to keep you apart.'

He looked wistful for a moment and I wondered if that was because he was sad for me or himself, so I asked him about Naomi.

He shrugged. 'I felt pretty cut up about the break-up at the time. I thought we had something really special but … you have to move on, don't you?' He didn't seem to want to say too much so I decided not to push it. He smiled. 'And we have moved on, haven't we?'

I leant over and kissed him by way of reply.

The only thing I didn't tell him about was Keira. As I was going to sleep that night, I asked myself why not. I knew he'd be supportive. But part of me didn't want to taint the image I hoped that he had of me of a positive person, someone who was a survivor. Kiera made me feel like a loser. She made me doubt myself and I didn't want to pass any of that on to Connor.

*

Pia and I decided to have a girlie afternoon on Saturday and we headed for one of our favourite spots – Westfield shopping mall. I'd talked things over with Dad and agreed to put two-thirds of what I'd earned over the summer into a savings account; the rest I had permission to spend as I liked. Pia and I didn't waste any time making arrangements and headed off early in the morning.

As we got on the bus, I found myself checking the street for Kiera. *Chill out*, I told myself. *Even if she has been hanging about the apartment block lately, she'd never be up this early on a Saturday!* I focused back on Pia and decided that I wasn't going to let Keira ruin my day.

'I've really liked being a PA,' I said as the bus chugged off. 'I've been thinking I might even like to do it as a job when I leave school or uni. I've enjoyed thinking about what to write to make the events sound fun and interesting, plus it has the added bonus of paying so well.'

'Yeah. I think you'd be good at it,' said Pia. 'Maybe you've found your vocation.'

'Maybe. I want to do some sort of writing, that's for sure. Working for Stephanie's shown me that much. What about you?'

'I think I'd like to start my own business,' she said. 'All this holiday work has shown me that I'm not sure I want to be the one being told what to do. I'd much rather be the one doing the telling.'

I laughed. 'Yeah, figures. You were born to be a boss.'

Pia biffed my arm. 'You saying I'm bossy?'

'Er . . . how can I put this? You know what you want and aren't afraid to go for it.'

'You mean bossy,' said Pia. 'See you would be good as a PA because you can be very diplomatic.'

'OK. But you said bossy, not me.'

It felt good to have some time with Pia doing our usual stuff, chatting about nothing in particular, winding each other up and having a laugh. Both of us had been caught up in our own lives lately and I felt like I'd hardly seen her. 'Whatever we do though, P, let's promise to always make time for each other, not get sucked into a career or relationship.'

'*Just* what I was going to say to you,' said Pia.

'And that's why we're good friends,' I replied.

We saw that we had reached our stop and got up to get off the bus. 'And by the way, I want to get you something today. A pressie.'

'I'm a working girl too,' she said. 'I can pay my way.'

'Bossy and proud,' I said.

'That's me. But you can buy me a cappuccino.'

Although I still wanted to get her something, I didn't push it because I didn't want to rub in the fact that I'd earned almost five times more than she had in the time I'd worked for Stephanie. *I wonder if Alisha used to feel this way?* I asked myself as we headed across the street to the mall. *Maybe it's easier to give than receive?* Now that I had some money, I wanted to buy something for JJ and Alisha too, a gesture in return for the endless gifts they'd brought me since I'd known them. My thoughts about giving presents or not soon disappeared when we got into Westfield and saw all the inviting window displays and signs promising *everything half price* or *best bargains of the year*. It felt great to go from shop to shop trying things on or stopping for a drink and knowing that we could pay for it all ourselves and still have money over.

I hugged myself and did a small skip. 'You know what, Pia? I haven't felt so happy in ages. Life is good. Things are going great with Connor. I'm starting to have a better idea of what I want to do when I leave school. Things are looking up. At the beginning of the summer, I felt like life was over, with JJ leaving and nothing going to plan. It had seemed so hopeless, but now life is good.'

'Everything changes,' said Pia. 'Hey, you're clearer about what job you might like to do but have you done any work on the what makes you happy part of the project lately?'

I shook my head. 'A bit here and there. I've been too busy *being* happy and finding out who I am.'

'Me too,' said Pia. 'Do you think Mrs Callahan will buy that as an excuse?'

I laughed. 'Doubt it.'

'Are you going to tell JJ about Connor?' she asked.

'When the time is right,' I replied.

'How would you feel if you knew he was seeing someone else?'

'Not sure. I still think about him a lot, but I know I have to let him go. He's on the other side of the world and I have to get on with my life over here. It's sad but Connor has taken some of the ache away and shown me that I can move on.'

Pia nodded. 'I'm glad and you never know, one day you might see JJ again.'

'I hope so,' I said. 'It's all down to timing some-times, I guess.'

Next stop was Banana Republic and just as I was

taking a pile of clothes into the changing room, my mobile rang. I quickly put the clothes down on the stool and took the call. It was Connor. He sounded weird.

'You OK?' I asked him. 'You sound different. Upset. Has something happened?'

Connor was quiet for a few moments. 'Yes. Something's happened, Jess. I . . . We need to talk.'

Something about the way he said those last four words hit me hard. We need to talk. Somehow I knew that I wasn't going to like what he had to say.

Happiness is:
A day in the Mall with your favourite girlfriend, some money in your pocket and permission to spend.
Late summer evenings in the garden holding hands with a boy you like, talking about your most private thoughts and knowing he is there for you and feeling trust starting to grow.

Unhappiness is:
When a boy phones and says in an unhappy voice, we need to talk.

18

Changes

After the call, I had no enthusiasm for carrying on shopping. My whole world had just come crashing down around me and I wanted to go home, crawl under my duvet and hide.

'What exactly did he say?' asked Pia as we headed for the exit of the mall.

'He saw Naomi last night. She showed up where he lived after I'd gone. She wants to give things another go.'

Pia sighed heavily. 'But I thought she was history. Connor told you that.'

'I know. That's what I don't understand.' I felt

numb. Like I'd left my body and was watching it from up on the roof. The mall that only minutes earlier seemed like the best place in the world suddenly felt overcrowded with unfriendly people pushing and shoving. Connor and I were over. I couldn't take it in. He said he felt he 'owed' it to Naomi to give their relationship another chance. What about me? Didn't he owe anything to me? I guess not. Had I just been a quick holiday affair to him and he *had* been on the rebound? It was so confusing. We'd felt so close when we cried together, held each other. We had made plans for the autumn. A future together. Did that all mean nothing? 'Actually I do understand,' I said. 'I've always known how much Naomi meant to him and how tough their break-up had been. I just never expected her to come back.'

'If they had problems before, there may be problems again,' said Pia. 'Why did she break up with him in the first place?'

'She felt it was too early to settle down into a serious relationship,' I replied.

'Ah,' said Pia. 'That means she wanted to play the field a bit, has done just that, probably kissed a few frogs and discovered that princes like Connor are the exception and so she wants to reclaim him. But don't forget she hurt him. Sometimes it's hard to let go of that and trust again.' I knew she was trying to tell me that there was hope, like she did when JJ had left, trying to say that it's not over for ever, but Connor breaking up with me was different to JJ. Connor breaking up with me made me realise that I had been second best for him all along. And that sucked.

Pia and I managed to get home without me blubbing in public, and as we hurried around to the back of Porchester Park, who was standing there but Keira – and she wasn't alone. She was with two other tall blonde girls who were leaning on the wall, smoking.

'This day just gets worse and worse,' I said as I stepped off the pavement to avoid them. Pia didn't though. She marched straight up to Keira. 'What are you doing here?' she asked.

Keira sneered down her nose. 'It's a free country.'

'Who's the midget?' asked one of Keira's friends.

'Oh, nobody,' Kiera replied.

This made me mad. 'Pia is not a nobody and she's not a midget.'

Keira turned her attention to me. 'Oh, Princess Perfect speaks,' she said.

'Leave her alone, this isn't the time,' said Pia and she pulled me towards the gate into the staff area.

'No hurry,' Keira called after me. 'We'll be waiting.'

'Oh, get a life,' said Pia.

Keira cracked up. 'How very original, darling. Don't worry, we have got lives, our own lives. We don't leech off the rich like you two do.'

'I'm going to call the police,' said Pia.

Keira burst out laughing. 'And say what? There are three teenage girls standing in a street? Have we done anything? I don't think so. Go ahead.'

Pia looked like she was going to punch Keira. I pulled her inside. 'She's not worth it,' I said as the gate swung open and we went inside.

'Tell your dad,' she said. 'Tell someone. It's seriously creepy the way she's been hanging around.'

'So you knew?'

Pia nodded. 'I didn't want to say anything because I didn't want you to worry. I'd already decided I was going to go out and give her a piece of my mind. We have to take action of some sort.'

I nodded but my head was still spinning from the call from Connor. Dealing with Keira and her nastiness was the last thing I felt like doing.

*

When we got inside, my mobile bleeped that there was a text message. It was from Connor. R u OK? Call me, it said.

'Don't reply,' said Pia. 'You're upset. Jeez. He couldn't even tell you face to face. A phone call? A text? That's so cowardly. You deserve better. Are you OK?! Course you're not. I could kill him.'

I smiled weakly. 'I wasn't going to call him. I wouldn't know what to say, like, if he said he wanted to stay friends. I don't think I could do that, not after what I thought we had together. We were so much more than friends.'

In the next hour, Pia did everything she could to try and cheer me up. She made me tea, offered to do my nails, made me toast and jam, which I couldn't eat, and for her sake, I tried to be more cheerful than I felt. 'I'll be OK,' I promised her. 'I just need to get my head around it.'

As the day drew on, she had to go and do some errands for her mum. 'Come with me,' she said, 'I don't want to leave you alone.'

'I'm OK. Honest. And I kind of need to be alone. Think things over.'

'OK but call me if you need anything.'

'I will.'

After Pia had gone, I went up to my bedroom and lay on the bed. I still felt numb and was trying to take in the enormity of Connor's call. I stared at the ceiling for a few minutes and groaned. I hated how I was feeling, like part of me had turned to stone. I felt so heavy but at the same time, like I wasn't there. I didn't want to be me; there was such an ache deep inside. I wanted – needed – to get away from it. Anything to distract me. I got up and went over to my laptop at my desk.

No such luck of escaping because there was an email from Connor.

Dear Jess,

I know it's a cliché, but it's not you, it's me. You're lovely and special and I feel bad if I have hurt you. But I can't deny what I have with Naomi. When we met up last night, the connection was still there and I can't lie to you about that. I feel I owe it to her – and to me – to try and make things work. I'm so sorry, Jess. I really like you, you know that. I think it was just bad timing, I wasn't over her. Not really. I tried to kid myself but . . . Call me. Please. Although I am sure I deserve it if you say you never want to see me or talk to me again, I want to

know that you're OK. I do care about you and I
hope that maybe, some time, we can be friends.
Connor x

Arghhhhhhhh, I thought. There it was. The 'I hope
that we can be friends' line. *Bad timing*, he said. That
seemed to be the explanation for everything. I
groaned again and Dave looked up from the bed.

'Boys do your head in, Dave,' I told him.

'Meow,' he said, put his head down and went back
to sleep.

I read and reread Connor's email. I called Pia and
told her about it.

'Should I email back and ask him to give me some
time?' I said. 'I feel like I'm reeling.'

'No. I still think you should wait,' said Pia. 'Don't
let him know how upset you are. A dignified silence
is what's needed until you're completely ready. Boys
are never very good with us girls when we're feeling
emotional. Wait until you're your usual self, by
which time he may have even come to his senses
and realised that he's just blown it with an amazing
girl.'

'OK. I'll wait,' I said.

After we'd finished our call, I still felt at a loss as to

what to do with myself. Pia was right. It would be best to wait until I felt clearer and I felt relieved that was what she'd advised. At the moment, I didn't know what I thought or felt, it was all a jumble in my head. Angry, sad, hurt, resilient – I will survive . . . and in the middle of it, a longing to see JJ, have his arms around me and feel the certainty I had with him that I was always his number one. He'd chosen me and there was never any girl from his past waiting in the wings. *I* was his girl from the past.

I glanced over at a photo by my bed. It was of Mum and me wearing silly Christmas hats, taken long before she got ill. I groaned again. I longed to see her too, talk to her, have her put her arms around me and tell me that everything would be all right. *Why do the people I love most go away?* I thought as a sudden wave of loss hit me. I so wanted to be with someone who cared about me. I thought about Dad, then remembered he was at a conference today. *Gran*, I thought. *I'll go to her.* Charlie and I lived at her house just after Mum died. I still loved visiting there because with all the familiar clutter collected over the years, it actually feels more like home than the mews house at Porchester Park. I feel connected to Mum there. Gran had photos of her all over the place and we'd spent so much time there when we were little, having Sunday lunches, sleepovers, Gran teaching Chaz and I how to cook, to draw, to read, then later, how to survive without Mum. Yes, Gran's would be the perfect place to go to.

I grabbed a jacket and headed for the side gate then did an about-turn in case Bully Girl and her mean mates were still outside. I really didn't want another encounter with them. I made my way through from the staff area to the main part of Porchester Park and crossed reception. Yoram was in his usual position by the door. I felt torn. I knew that I wasn't supposed to use the front entrance, apart from when I was with a resident, but I didn't want to go out the back way either. The wrath of Yoram or an encounter with Keira? Which was worse? I went over to Yoram. He gave me his usual unfriendly stare and I almost backed away. *This is ridiculous*, I thought. *I can't even set foot outside my own home.*

I took a deep breath and went over to him. 'Er . . . hi, Yoram. I wondered if I could possibly go out the front today?'

Yoram's eyes narrowed. 'I think you know the rules, Jess.'

I sighed. 'I do. Staff and family of staff have to use

the side entrance. Can't there be exceptions some-times?'

'Then the rules would be pointless,' he replied.

I sighed heavily and turned to go back inside. 'Never mind. I'll go out the side then.'

'Why do you want to go out the front?' Yoram called after me. 'That girl been hanging about again?'

I turned back to him. 'Yes she has and that's why I don't want to go out the side. I've tried asking her to go away. She just laughed at me.'

Yoram stared at me hard. 'You got to toughen up, Jess. Got to learn to stand up for yourself. Fight your battles.'

'Or not when there's three of them,' I said. Got to learn to fight your battles? I felt like thumping him. I felt a sudden fist of anger in the pit of my stomach. *I've been dumped by Connor and am a love loser. I'm trapped in my own home because of Keira. And Yoram's telling me to toughen up. He doesn't understand. No-one understands. Well, I've had enough. I am tough! And I won't be a prisoner scared to leave my own bedroom because of Keira. I can't – won't – let her run my life.*

'Does your father know about this girl?' Yoram asked.

'He's away on a conference today. And anyway, I

don't go running to him all the time like a baby,' I said. 'I can handle Keira.'

'Keira, huh? That's her name? Good for you,' said Yoram. 'Show her who you are.'

Love loser, prisoner, reject, second best, victim, that's who I am, said a negative part of my mind. I looked at Yoram. 'Show her who I am? OK. So who am I?'

'You're a good kid,' said Yoram.

I laughed. '*Kid?* I'll be sixteen in December.'

'Yes,' said Yoram. 'Kid. A good kid.'

'I always thought you disapproved of me.'

'Why would you think that?' He tapped his nose. 'I keep what I think private. But it's my business to watch people. I get to see who is who and who's made of what. I've seen you around. Watched how you've adapted to living here. I know you're not a pushover, that's for sure. You're a star. A superstar. If you were my daughter, I'd be proud of you.'

I almost fell over. Yoram had paid me a compliment. 'Are you on drugs, Yoram?

For the first time since I'd moved to Porchester Park, Yoram smiled – well almost, more like a glimmer of one. 'No, Jess. I am most certainly not on drugs.'

'So can I go out the front?'

'If I make an exception for you, I'll have to make an exception for everyone.'

I felt like kicking something. *Life is so frustrating sometimes*, I thought as I went back in through the reception area, back out to the staff houses, then to the side gate. To go out and face Kiera or to slope back home and hide in my bedroom until the coast is clear? Yoram's words played in my head. *You're not a pushover. You're a good kid. Stand up for yourself.* I had to tell Pia what he'd said. She'd die with shock. I quickly texted. Guess what? Yoram just told me I am a SUPERSTAR!

She texted back. I always nu. Just bn w8ng 4 u 2 c it. Call u l8r. Got 2 go. XXX

I stared at the gate and wondered what lay on the other side. I turned my face up to the sky. 'Arghhhhhhhh,' I groaned. No way out the front, no way out the side. What was I suppose to do? Chicken out?

Once again, I felt the fist of anger in my stomach. Angry with Connor for making me feel this way. Angry with Naomi for ruining everything. Angry with Keira for being a total bitch to me. How dare Keira come into my life and make it miserable? I had done *nothing* to her. Maybe she would have moved on from outside, maybe not. I didn't care anymore and the feeling was liberating. In the meantime, I felt fired up.

I am a star. A *SUPERstar*, I told myself as I punched in the gate exit code and it swung open. I took a deep breath, threw my shoulders back and stepped onto the pavement. I was ready to face Keira. Wherever she was, I wasn't going to let her intimidate me anymore.

<u>Who am I?</u>
A survivor. A superstar.

<u>Happiness is:</u>
Someone unexpected paying you a fab compliment.

19

Confrontation

'Let's make a list,' said Gran after I'd brought her up to date on all my news about JJ, Connor and Keira. We were lying on opposite sofas with our feet up on the arm rests, having just had tea, and Marmite on toast. Yum. One of my favourites. Gran was wearing jeans and a lovely peacock-blue velvet top. She's such a groovy gran. With silver-white hair cut into a neat bob, she looks bohemian but elegant too. I was feeling so much better for spilling out to her the whole Connor and Keira story, and also feeling good that I hadn't chickened out and stayed at home.

'What kind of list?' I asked.

'A wish list for your perfect boy.'

I laughed. This was the sort of thing I did with my mates but then Gran was one of my best friends as well as my grandmother. 'OK.'

She got up and got a piece of paper and a pen, then looked at me. 'Shoot.'

I thought for a few moments and Connor's face came into my mind. 'A boy for whom I am number one.'

Gran wrote that down. 'Good. And what would he look like?'

'Tall because I'm tall and I like a boy who can look me in the eye. I don't mind hair or colour of eyes or skin, but I do like a boy to be reasonably good-looking, but not so much that he's full of himself. There's a boy like that at our school, Tom, and I was into him for a while but soon realised I could never be number one for him because his number one was always going to be himself.'

Gran laughed. 'I know the type.'

'I'd like a boy with a good sense of humour. That's very important. Someone generous and kind. Has goals. Stuff he wants to achieve. I liked that about Connor. He was so passionate about his photography. I don't like boys who are too needy or possessive.'

Gran nodded and continued writing. 'Not needy.'

'A boy who's open about his feelings. Not someone who's moody. Or angry. Fun to be with but cares about the environment. Oh and must like animals.'

'Absolutely,' Gran agreed. 'Very important. Anything else?'

I thought for a bit longer and then sighed.

'What's the sigh for?'

'I realised I've just described JJ.'

'OK, I have one for you,' said Gran. 'Doesn't live in another continent.'

'Exactly,' I said. 'Skype and having a cyber-boyfriend just doesn't do it. I do miss JJ, though, and he always made me feel like I was so important in his life.'

'You never know who's around the next corner,' said Gran.

'Keira lately,' I said. I meant it as a joke but Gran didn't laugh.

'Have you told your father about her?'

I shook my head. 'It's my problem and he has enough to deal with at Porchester Park without hearing Keira's outside.'

'Oh, Jess. He'd want to know. He's your father. He cares about you as I do and wouldn't want to think you're being bullied.'

'I'll sort it, Gran. I will.'

'I hope so because this actually bothers me more than your love life. I remember Keira well,' she said. 'She was often round when you lived down the road. I remember her because I never really liked her, and it's unusual that I don't like a child, but there was something mean about her. I caught her watching the other children play on a number of occasions and she had a hard look in her eye, like she was working out some plan instead of just enjoying being there like the rest of you.'

'Well, she's not going to ruin my life anymore,' I said, then sighed. 'It's been ruined enough.' The thought that I wouldn't be seeing Connor anymore hit me again. 'Oh, Gran, Connor and I had so many plans for the autumn, exhibitions we were going to see—'

'You can still do those things,' said Gran. 'I'll come with you. Don't let not having a boyfriend prevent you from doing anything. Yes, it's nice to have someone special to share things with but it's important to not be dependent on just one person for your happiness. Strangely, if you can do that, you'll find that makes you all the more attractive.'

'Connor's left a few messages but I don't feel like talking yet,' I said.

'Then don't,' said Gran. 'He's made his choice and you don't have to give him your blessing. So, do you want to have dinner and stay over?'

'Could I?' I looked around at the comfy clutter that was Gran's house. I felt utterly safe there. 'I'd love it and do you think we could invite Charlie and Aunt Maddie too? I'll help you cook. It's been ages since we had a family meal.'

'Good idea,' said Gran. 'I'll do your favourite roast chicken even though it's not Sunday.' She looked at me with such fondness. 'Boys may come and go, but your family will always be here.' She went quiet for a few moments. I knew we were both thinking the same thing – except for Mum. She glanced up and gave me a sad smile. Gran and I often had a telepathic bond.

The next morning I set off back to Porchester Park feeling a lot more positive. Charlie had been straight round when he'd realised that Gran was cooking. He loved a good meal and although Dad hired a lady to come in and cook for us in the term time, he hadn't felt it was necessary in the holidays because none of us were ever sure what we were doing and whether we'd be home. Hence, we lived on simple, quick meals that we threw together, takeaways or toasties.

Aunt Maddie had come round to Gran's too and we'd all had a good laugh and catch-up around the table. Afterwards, because it was lovely balmy night, we sat out in Gran's garden drinking milky coffees and talking about nothing in particular. When Charlie had gone back to Porchester Park and Aunt Maddie back to her flat, I'd curled up on the sofa with Gran and we'd watched a couple of episodes of *Miranda* (Gran's favourite sit-com). I felt cosy, content and thankful for my family.

My head was totally somewhere else when I got off the bus at my stop. I was thinking that I must add *time with family* to my happiness list as I strode round the corner, heading for the side gate, and smack into Keira and her mates.

'Hey, watch where you're going,' said Keira and she shoved me in the chest with the fingers on both hands. She had long nails and it hurt.

'Whoops,' I said and stepped aside and away from her. *Remember, remember*, I told myself. *She doesn't intimidate me.* 'I didn't mean to walk into you.'

Keira sneered. 'Apologetic as well as stupid,' she said to her friends who came forward and closed around me. They started simpering and saying, 'Sorry, sorry,' in pathetic voices.

I tried to get out of the circle they were forming around me. 'Hey, let me go. There are three of you.'

'Dere are dree of you,' Keira droned in a mocking girlie tone. She grabbed my hair and yanked it back.

'Ow,' I said and I put my hand up to try and release myself. I could feel my heart beating hard in my chest and it was difficult to catch my breath. All I could see was the girls' faces closing in on me and smell nicotine on their breath. I tried to push them aside, but there was no way I could deal with all of them. I ducked down to try and get out from under their arms, but they just laughed and began to push and shove me.

Two large hands came out of nowhere and grabbed two of the girls. It was Yoram and he pulled them away from me as if they weighed nothing. A second pair of hands grabbed Keira. It was Didier. Both he and Yoram were wearing their shades and their smart suits.

'Get the Men in Black,' Keira jeered at them, though her two friends had both gone pale.

Yoram let the girls go and put his face close to Keira's. 'So you're Keira, the ringleader of this little party, are you?'

'Might be.'

He got out a camera and snapped her photo. 'For

your information, Keira, I've taken a few snaps already of you and your friends and I've taken note of all the times and days you've been here.'

'Stalker,' said Keira. 'I could report you to the police for photographing young girls.'

'They already know. I work very closely with the police.'

Keira's friends paled even more and looked around as if searching for an escape.

'I think they'll be very interested in your activities lately,' Yoram continued, 'and the fact that your presence here is not only intimidating to one of our residents, but you're close to private property. The police may like to know what your intentions here are.'

'Oh shut up,' said Keira but she looked slightly less confident. 'And what are they going to do?'

'You OK, Jess?' asked Didier.

'You OK, Jess?' mocked Keira in the tone she had used earlier.

'Yes, fine, thank you.'

'So Jess is OK,' said Keira. 'Can we go now?'

'No, you can't,' said Yoram. 'I think we need to have a little chat.' He pointed at one of Keira's friends. 'Grace O'Neill. Seven Northern Road.'

She gasped. 'How do you know that?'

Yoram didn't reply. He turned to the next girl. 'Marie Wilson. White Cottage, Harford Road.'

She also looked shocked.

'And finally, Keira. You're at five hundred and sixty-seven, Wilmslow Street, Hammersmith.' He made the gesture that Keira had made to me only weeks ago, two fingers up to the eyes then he pointed those fingers at Keira. 'Yes. I know where you live. And yes, I will be watching you, but you won't know it.'

'You don't scare me,' said Keira.

Yoram stood very close to her. He took off his shades and looked directly at her. 'Think again,' he said. 'You might find that you change your mind about that.' She tried to stare back at him but after a while, she looked away, down at the pavement. 'My friend here and I are both ex-SAS and take the protection of our residents very seriously. Keira, don't ever use that tone when speaking to an adult again. This is a warning. You only get one. Now get out of here and if I ever see you hanging around here again, I, my friend here and the police will take action. Have you got that?'

The girls nodded.

'And, Keira, I suggest that you don't ever try to contact Jess again by phone or Facebook. Don't forget I know where each one of you lives and how to find you. Now, get out of here before I change my mind and have you locked up and believe me, I could do that. We don't even have to go to the police, we have our own lock-up at Porchester Park.'

The girls didn't need to be told twice and scarpered fast.

'How did you know about Facebook and the texts?' I asked Yoram.

He tapped his nose. 'It's my business to know everything that goes on in Porchester Park.'

'And do we really have a lock-up room?'

Didier grinned. 'Of course not, but they don't know that.'

'Now,' said Yoram. 'The next few weekends. Saturday mornings. What are you doing?'

'Oh, schoolwork probably as we start back in a week. Maybe a bit of time chilling. Usual stuff.'

'Wrong,' said Yoram. 'You and Pia will meet me or Didier in the apartment's gym. You can bring your brother too.'

'What for?'

'Self-defence classes,' he said. 'Didier and I will give

you some pointers to make sure you can look after yourself in the future.'

They both sprang into martial art positions and play fought. I'd never seen them larking about like that.

'Ten o'clock sharp, next Saturday,' said Yoram as he sprang back.

The gym is only for residents, I thought. *The rules are no staff are allowed to use the facilities*. I decided not to say that. Yoram was making an exception and I wasn't going to argue.

I saluted. 'Yes, sir! I'll be there!'

Yoram gave me a withering look. 'Don't push it, Hall,' he said.

I gave him a hug. It was like embracing a tree, he was so stiff. 'Thanks, Yoram. You're a real pal.' I turned to Didier and gave him a squeeze. He cuddled me back. I glanced at Yoram's face. He looked quite touched, but quickly assumed his unreadable expression.

'I mean it, thank you. I don't know what I'd have done without you today,' I said.

Yoram gently shoved me towards the side gate. 'You'd have been OK. You're tougher than you think. Now go inside and take it easy.'

20

Moving On

I never did call Connor back, and after a while his texts stopped. I didn't want to hear his voice, I thought it would hurt too much, but I did send an email saying that I wished him happiness. I did. He was a nice guy and maybe it was a question of right boy, wrong time. Which seemed to be the story of my life. Sad for me but there was little I could do about it and after a few crying sessions, I picked myself up and moved on.

I didn't hear from Keira again either after the day Yoram had confronted her and I also noticed that she had taken herself off Facebook. I wouldn't have cared if she'd stayed on. I'd never let someone like her bother me so much again.

'So I'll be starting school as a single girl,' I said to Pia the next day as we sat in her lounge. I'd brought my happiness notebook ready to write up my thoughts from the summer. 'And Stephanie says the future's looking good for me. I have Gemini rising which means I am a good communicator and apparently loads of people who write and who are in publishing or journalism are either Gemini or have Gemini rising, so that looks good for me pursuing writing as a career option. Stephanie also said I can expect the unexpected when it comes to romance. So, it's all looking good.'

'Do you believe in astrology totally now?' Pia asked.

I shrugged. 'Well, Stephanie said you can't let it rule your life, you still have to go out and make things happen. I think the stars can give you some guidance as to what to expect – like a bumpy patch or a star-studded phase. She said my horoscope shows things are going to get better after a bumpy time, especially romantically.'

'Well, that's good,' Pia said. 'And you're in a great position to start the Sixth Form. I'd envy your new single status if I didn't like Henry so much. You know that there will be loads of new boys from other schools come to do their A-levels. New term, new possibilities.'

I put the back of my hand up to my forehead and said in my best Shakespearian accent, 'Mine is a high and lonely destiny and in the end ...' (I paused for dramatic effect) 'it is better to have loved and lost than never to have loved at all.'

Pia threw a cushion at me. 'You're not even sixteen yet. You have a whole load of relationships ahead of you and will have boys queuing up for you once they know you're free.'

'Maybe but I don't want just any old boy. JJ was really special and Connor was too. I miss them both. Love isn't always easy, is it?'

Pia shook her head, though she didn't look very convinced. She and Henry seemed to have a really easy time.

'No one's ever happy, are they?' I commented. 'You're jealous of me starting Sixth Form free and single and I envy you because your boyfriend is close by.'

Pia glanced down at our notebooks. 'I think happiness is all in the head. It's a state of mind, that's my conclusion. It's not a situation that makes you happy, it's how you react to it.'

'True that,' I said and wrote down what she'd said.

When I got home, I turned on my computer to edit my happiness ideas and the Skype phone rang.

It was JJ. 'Hey, cyber-girl.'

'Hey, cyber-boy.'

He looked great, better than I'd seen him for ages, like a weight had lifted off his shoulders. 'How you doing?' he asked.

'So so. You?'

'Just so.'

I laughed. 'God, I miss you, JJ.'

'Me too. Miss you, I mean.'

'You seem very chirpy.'

'Yeah. I'm feeling better than I have in a while. Gramps is much more stable now. He even got out of bed a few days ago and is mobile again. The doctors are really pleased with his progress.'

I suddenly noticed the room he was calling from. It looked very familiar . . .

'Your room over there looks like your room here.'

JJ grinned. 'Guess why that is?'

'Same decorator?'

JJ shook his head. 'Nope.'

'Why then?'

'Because it *is* my room here. Mom wanted to come over to check a few things and see Stephanie so I'm back with her.'

I gasped. 'No way. So you're here in the UK?'

JJ nodded. 'I am. I wanted to surprise you. I'm here for a week.'

'A week?'

'Yep. And I believe you have just a week before term starts.'

'I do, term starts a bit later than the other years because I'll be going into Sixth Form.'

'You got any plans?'

'Nope.'

'So. Let's not waste any time. See you in five?'

'Make that two and a half. I'll meet you halfway!'

Twenty minutes later, I was curled up on the sofa up in the Lewises' apartment. Mrs Lewis and Stephanie were out for the afternoon so it was just JJ and me. After chatting and catching up, we just sat, basking in the lovely feeling of being back together. It was pure heaven.

'Do you feel it too?' asked JJ.

'I do,' I replied.

'It's been a funny old summer,' he said as he pulled me in closer to him.

I laughed. 'Understatement. Not what I had in mind at all. Not any of it.'

'What's that saying? Life is what happens to you while you're busy making plans.'

'Makes sense,' I replied.

'But here we are,' he said. 'Still together.'

'Yes but—'

JJ leant over and kissed me, a really long deep kiss. When we drew apart, he looked right into my eyes and I felt the connection we'd always had. 'No buts,' he said. 'You're part of my life, Jess Hall, and though I tried to let you go, I've realised that I don't want to. We'd only just got started and there we were saying goodbye. It just didn't feel right. I feel we owe it to each other to see where this thing takes us.'

'But you'll be in the US and I'll be over here.'

'There are holidays and … I spoke to Mom. She knows how I feel about you. If you're willing and haven't met anyone else, I'd like to come over when I can and Mom said you can visit us.' He paused a moment and looked anxious. 'You haven't met anyone else, have you?'

'I ...' I wasn't sure whether to tell him about Connor. It didn't feel like the right time. 'I tried to put a wall up and block out my feelings for you,' I said. 'It was too painful to think I wouldn't be seeing you again or sitting here like this. But I can assure you, there are no other boys in my life and you will always be my number one.' It was the truth. I might tell him about Connor at a later date because I didn't want there to be any secrets between us. But for now, what was there to tell? I'd lost my way for a while but now I was back where I belonged, in JJ's arms.

JJ grinned then reached over to the coffee table and picked up an envelope. 'In that case, I want to give you an early birthday present. It's from all of us. Mom, Pop, Alisha and me.'

I took the envelope. 'Can I open it now?'

JJ nodded so I ripped the envelope open. 'Oh my God!' It was a return ticket to America for the half-term holiday.

'Like it?' asked JJ.

'*Love* it,' I said. 'It's the best birthday present ever.'

Project for Mrs Callahan
Jess Hall's Thoughts on Happiness

<u>Snapshot moments of happiness from the summer</u>
* Being with family at Gran's, eating and chatting.
* Being with my cat, Dave, as well as having long conversations with him.
* Sitting on a train, staring out of the window as the world flashes by.
* A sweet dog giving me his paw to say hello.

* Flirting with a boy and feeling that there are possibilities.
* Sinking your teeth into a warm, freshly baked cookie.
* Being tucked up on a sofa with my little cousins who are fresh from their bath and smell of soap, watching kids' TV with them and eating crisps.
* Sitting on a beach at sunset in a warm breeze, looking out to sea.
* Doing the mop dance with Pia.
* Getting good GCSE results and sharing the news with friends who've done the same.
* Being given an airline ticket for the half-term holidays to go and visit my boyfriend and his family in the States.

Happiness is contrast:
* To get warm when you've been cold, cool down when you've been hot.
* A lie-in when you've had a run of early mornings.
* Time off when you've been busy –

like the feeling on the last Friday of
term. Yay.
* A project when you've been bored.
* A boy you didn't think you were
going to see again turning up to
surprise you. Double yay.

Happiness is being with the right boy
who gets you.

Happiness is knowing that friends and
family are well and happy.

Happiness is a state of mind.

Best of all, happiness is time spent
with great mates (boys included) who
are there for you and you for them.
That has to be the best feeling in the
world.

Who am I?
A Sagittarian.
A bundle of changing and evolving
feelings.

A loyal friend who is thoughtful about others.
I like writing and would like to pursue this as a career.

Two lessons I've learnt over the summer:
Everything changes.
Never say never.